WELL HUNG

by Lauren Blakely

ALSO BY LAUREN BLAKELY

The Caught Up in Love Series (Each book in this series follows a different couple so each book can be read separately, or enjoyed as a series since characters crossover)

Caught Up in Her (A short prequel novella to *Caught Up in Us*)
Caught Up In Us
Pretending He's Mine
Trophy Husband
Stars in Their Eyes

Standalone Novels

BIG ROCK
Mister O
Well Hung
The Sexy One (Oct 2016)
Full Package (Jan 2017)
Joy Stick (Spring 2017)
Far Too Tempting
21 Stolen Kisses
Playing With Her Heart (A standalone SEDUCTIVE NIGHTS spin-off novel about Jill and Davis)

The No Regrets Series

The Thrill of It
The Start of Us
Every Second With You

The Seductive Nights Series

First Night (Julia and Clay, prequel novella)
Night After Night (Julia and Clay, book one)
After This Night (Julia and Clay, book two)
One More Night (Julia and Clay, book three)
A Wildly Seductive Night (Julia and Clay novella)
Nights With Him (A standalone novel about Michelle and Jack)
Forbidden Nights (A standalone novel about Nate and Casey)

The Sinful Nights Series

Sweet Sinful Nights
Sinful Desire
Sinful Longing
Sinful Love

The Fighting Fire Series

Burn For Me (Smith and Jamie)
Melt for Him (Megan and Becker)
Consumed By You (Travis and Cara)

The Jewel Series

The Sapphire Affair
The Sapphire Heist

ABOUT

Here's what you need to know about me—I'm well-off, well-hung and quick with a joke. Women like a guy who makes them laugh—and I don't mean at the size of his d*ck. No, they want their funny with a side of huge... not to mention loyal. I've got all that plus a big bank account, thanks to my booming construction business. Yup. I know how to use all my tools.

Enter Natalie. Hot, sexy, smart, and my new assistant. Which makes her totally off limits... Hey, I'm a good guy. Really. I do my best to stay far away from the kind of temptation she brings to work.

Until one night in Vegas... Yeah, you've heard this one before. Bad news on the business front, drowning our sorrows in a few too many Harvey Wallbangers, and then I'm banging her. In my hotel room. In her hotel room. Behind the Titanic slot machine at the Flamingo (don't ask). And before I can make her say "Oh God right there YES!" one more time, we're both saying yes—the big yes—at a roadside chapel in front of a guy in press-on sideburns and a shiny gold leisure suit.

But it turns out what happened in Vegas didn't stay in Vegas. And now, my dick doesn't stay in my pants when she's around. I try to resist. Honest. But the more we try to keep our hands to ourselves, the more we end up naked again, and the more time I want to spend with her fully clothed, too.

The question now is…do I take this woman to be my ex-wife?

PROLOGUE

Once upon a time, there was a guy, there was a girl, and some crazy shit went down.

The end.

.

.

.

.

.

.

.

Just messing with you.

I'm a full-service kind of guy, and I'd never skip the good part. When I tell a you'll-never-believe-what-happened kind of story, I'll stamp it with my personal guarantee that you're getting the whole Oreo, from the delicious chocolate wafers to the sweet crème filling. And please, I encourage you to devour it all, every mouth-watering morsel of the tale.

Like that one time on the rollercoaster when we learned exactly why some people shriek at the top of their lungs on the downhill.

Or the tale of the quickie behind the lucky slot machine, when someone nailed three cherries while I nailed her.

Not sure either of those times topped the afternoon with the ladder, though.

What? You don't have any fantasies involving ladders? You will soon, and you'll never think of the top rung of a ladder the same way again.

But in between all of that so-insane-it-should-be-illegal stuff that I never could have predicted in my wildest imagination—and look, it's lawless up there between my ears—there was some seriously real shit, too.

The type of real that fucks your heart with a chainsaw.

That damn near rips it out of your chest.

That was what happened to me.

So now, after nearly sixty-nine days with her—and the irony of that number is most decidedly *not* lost on me—I'm *here.*

On the steps of the courthouse. She's going up. I'm going down.

I reach for her arm. Wrap my hand around it. "Is this how it ends?"

My voice barely sounds like my own.

Hers is a whisper, too. "You tell me."

I could tell you I'm a player. I could tell you I've got a big dick, a rock-hard body, and a heart of gold. But you're not here for my résumé. Besides, you've heard stories before of the player tamed.

You haven't heard this one.

Warning: I don't give spoilers, so you'll just need to buckle up and enjoy the ride.

The only thing I'll tell you is this—our ending is one you'll never see coming.

CHAPTER ONE

I'm going to let you in on a little secret about guys. When we see a chick we like, we all say she is hot for us. Doesn't matter who the woman is, what her situation might be, or if we even have a clue if it's true or not. We just say it.

Like right now.

Floyd, the redheaded dude who was three days late dropping off the hinges for this swank Upper East Side penthouse, has parked an elbow on the counter and is yammering away. Guess he needs a break from the hard work of missing a deadline. I'm determined to meet it though, so I keep working, screwing the hinges into the cabinet door for one of my clients.

A client who Floyd believes is *hot for his sausage*.

His words. Not mine.

"Wyatt, did you see the way Lila stared at me when I walked in?" he says as he grabs his black and green energy drink, pounds it, then swipes his hand over his mouth, leaving a trail of droplets on his red-flecked goatee.

"Hmm. I must have missed that moment," I say, and I'm glad that Lila is downstairs in the building's gym right now and can't hear him.

"I'm telling you, the chicks just line up for me at every job," Floyd says, puffing out his chest.

I arch an eyebrow as I twist the screwdriver and give him my best deadpan retort. "This line of women—would you say it extends beyond the door and down the hallway of every client's home?"

He nods, like he buys his own bullshit. Evidently, sarcasm is lost on the Hot Sausage King.

"Absolutely. I could have them all day long. One right after the other. That's why we're in this business, right, bro?"

He holds up a fist for knocking, but my hands are busy, so I just say, "For the tail?"

He nods. "Best tail I've ever had. Nothing quite like a hammer in the hand to nab the chickadees."

I laugh at this incredible line of baloney. Because tail is exactly why I got into the home construction business. *Not.* "You'd probably never be tired, either? You've got constant stamina?" I ask, egging him on as I move to the next hinge, spacing it evenly along the back of the door.

"Oh yeah. But here's the thing. This is the golden rule of our business," he adds, then presses his finger to his lips.

Oh, lucky me. He's going to let me in on his secret.

"I love rules. Tell me, tell me," I say, like an eager acolyte.

"The golden rule is this—you can bang the clients, but you can't ever screw your assistant."

"That so?" I say in a completely serious voice, as if he's just dispensed wisdom from Mount Olympus.

Floyd nods sagely. "Trust me. Learn from my mistakes. I lost the best assistant in the universe when I couldn't keep my hands off her fine ass," he says, then sighs wistfully as his gaze drifts to the ceiling. He must be remembering her sweet cheeks. "A good assistant is worth her weight in gold." He taps his chest. "That's why my new one is a gray-haired granny. That just removes the temptation entirely."

I finish screwing the hinges to the door, and take the drill from my tool belt. Pointing it at him, I meet his eyes. "But consider this . . ." I let my voice trail off, take a pregnant pause, then say, "What if I was into silver foxes?"

His eyes widen, and his words come out dry and unsure. "You are?"

"Absolutely. I'm an equal-opportunity man." I can't resist yanking his chain, so I keep going, giving a big serving of braggart right back at him. "They float my boat, and let me tell you, the GILFs are hot for me. Talk about a line of hotties. Retirees as far as the eye can see. I can't keep my hands off them."

"You know it. Good thing you don't have a GILF manning your phones then, or you'd be royally fucked."

"Pun intended, right?" I set down the drill, rest the door on the counter, and lower my voice. "But you know, Floyd, there's another option," I say, and now it's my turn to lean in, lower my voice, and pass on my brilliance.

"Yeah?" He's practically salivating for what he no doubt thinks will be an office sex tip.

I straighten to my full height. I'm six two, and I tower over him. "You could"—I keep my tone even and light —"for instance"—I take a final beat—"keep your dick in your pants at work."

The entire penthouse goes silent. Floyd scratches his head. He furrows his brow and says, "Huh?"

Apparently, my advice is so foreign I might as well have been speaking Turkish. "Anyway, time to go, Floyd. I need to finish this job on time for Lila, who is neither hot for your sausage, nor your baloney."

I clap him on the back, thank him for the late delivery of hinges, and send him on his way.

A few hours later, I've finished my work for the day, just as a peppy Lila arrives home from her gym session, bouncing in her leggings and sneakers. I show her what I worked on this afternoon in her kitchen remodel, and update her on what needs to be done tomorrow as I move into the homestretch of the job.

"It's really coming together so nicely," she says in her perky way. "You do amazing work. And I'm so glad Natalie was able to fit this remodel work in your schedule. I know it was a tight squeeze, but you come so highly recommended, and I had to have the best for my home."

I nod and say thank you, then give credit where it's due. "Natalie is the wizard of scheduling. She can pretty much make anything work."

"Good, because I might have another project for you. Let me talk to my husband, Craig, when he gets home tonight from his board meeting, and then we'll set something up?"

"Sounds like a plan. And I'll see you tomorrow to finish the cabinets."

Soon I'm back at our office in the West 50s, dropping off tools and materials, and none other than the Mistress of Scheduling herself, aka the woman who turned this ship around, greets me.

"Hey, Wyatt," Natalie calls out from her desk as I walk in.

See, I almost want to call Floyd and tell him that following my advice is *easy*. I manage it every day. What a miracle. Especially considering I have a whip-smart assistant who's beautiful, clever, fantastic at her job, and has a smile that just slays me. Call me old-fashioned. I'm a sucker for a woman with a great smile, and Natalie, with her bright blue eyes and cheerleader blond hair, wins at smiling. She's the perfect, all-American girl, like an apple pie, and I just want to eat her up.

I mean, I don't want that.

Fuck, that came out wrong.

I totally don't want to eat my assistant. Or bang my assistant. Or bend my assistant over the desk.

See? I've followed my own advice. My dick is safely in my pants.

Besides, Natalie's great at her job, and it's just wrong to think of her that way. Not to mention dangerous. Last time I canoodled with someone I worked with, my business could have tanked. That experience taught me a lesson I should have learned a long time ago—don't mix business with pleasure. You'll get a nasty cocktail with a bitter aftertaste. So even though Natalie has the prettiest face I've seen in ages, and the most generous heart, topped by a complete goofball side, and even though I once thought she wanted me, I can't go there with her.

I keep it all fun and games when she flashes me that killer smile and asks, "How's the Mayweather job coming along?"

I gesture from my torso all the way down to my legs then sniff the air for effect. "Great, but do you have anything to get the scent of douche off me?"

She points to the shelves on the far wall of our office and deadpans, "Top shelf. Left side. I got a new anti-asshole spray last week. But it sometimes takes a few pumps to really work. So work it good, 'kay?"

I give her a thumbs-up, pretend to grab a can of aerosol and douse myself with it, then put it back. "There. All better."

I grab the ratty mustard-colored chair across from her desk and sink down in it. Clients don't come here; the office is just for us, so we can skimp on furniture.

She twirls the pen in her hand. "So who caused the contamination today? Was it Floyd or Kevin the oily electrician you tried to put a chokehold on?"

"Oily Kevin needed the chokehold. Agree or disagree?"

She nods. "Completely agree. There's so much agreement in me, I can't imagine how much more I could possibly agree."

"The chokehold was one hundred percent certifiably necessary," I add, since Kevin had hit on her when he stopped by a few weeks ago. Here's the thing—Natalie could dropkick him in the blink of an eye. She could slam him to the ground herself. But that shit he pulled with the leering and lewd comments does not fly with me. I would have done the same if a dude tried to get fresh with my little sister, Josie, at the bakery where she works. So I'd dropped a hand on Kevin's shoulder, Vulcan style, and promptly escorted him the fuck out of my office. No one, and I mean no one, gets to put the moves on my employees.

"It was Floyd today," I tell her, then give her the safe-for-work version of the story—the one about Floyd's client conquests, not his comments about banging assistants.

There's no need to have that hanging out there in the air between us. Can't plant that forbidden idea in her head.

That risky, dangerous, dirty, filthy, completely fucking alluring idea. My eyes roam the office briefly, and I catalogue all the places that are calling out to be christened. Her desk, her chair, the floor . . .

Just like that, my head is a wild rumpus of inappropriate ideas. Exactly what it shouldn't be. It's like horny aliens have invaded my mind.

But I'm not Floyd. I can do better, so I picture a vise, jam the images into it, and crush them out of my mind. The dirty images and the horny aliens, too.

"And then I escorted him out of Lila's home and said see ya later," I tell her, finishing the story, as I drag a hand through my dark brown hair. "Like, in another lifetime later."

"Hmm . . ." she says.

"Hmm, that's great, or hmm, why did I give one of our suppliers the heave-ho?"

"Hmm, as in your story gives me a good idea. Something I've wanted to do for a long time."

"What's that?"

Her eyes sparkle. Hers are a lighter shade than my dark blue. "Want me to find a new hinge supplier?"

The idea is beyond perfect. I smack my palm against the edge of her desk enthusiastically. "Yes. And for the record, you're brilliant and beauti—" I cut the last word off so it sounds like a low bass note. Note to self: Don't call her beautiful when you're berating other men for hitting on her at work.

She's watching me, waiting for me to finish my sentence, and somehow I twist the words into a new compliment, as I say, "Brilliant, and . . . bountiful."

Bountiful? Seriously? What the hell was that? Maybe she won't notice.

No such luck.

"Bountiful?" she asks, skepticism thick in her tone. As it fucking should be. "I'm bountiful?"

I nod, going with it, owning it. "Your brain. It's like a cornucopia of ideas. It's a Thanksgiving bounty. It's bountiful," I say, because I've got to sell this cover-up.

She squares her shoulders. "If you say so, Hammer. And this bountiful brain was two steps ahead today. I already found a new supplier. I called around, talked to some of our colleagues, and got some great recommendations. I already have a new hinge guy lined up."

My smile spreads quickly. "Damn. You are three steps ahead of me."

"A good assistant should be."

"And you're a great one. What do you say we go celebrate six months of you making WH Carpentry & Construction a much better business than it was before?"

WH stands for my name, Wyatt Hammer.

But WH also might stand for something else. You'll see. Don't worry. The whole Oreo, remember? I'll give it to you.

CHAPTER TWO

She chooses the vegetarian bibimbap, supernova spicy style, at a Korean restaurant off Ninth Avenue, not far from the office.

"Bibimbap," she says, like she's weighing the word. "It's challenging to pronounce and usually comes out like 'bippity-bop,' something a fairy godmother from a Disney movie says. But in fact, bibimbap tastes nothing like a Disney movie."

"Or like a fairy godmother," I add, stretching my neck to the side to work out the kinks in it from today's job. Eight hours on my feet, screwing, pounding and drilling. Nothing like a hard day's work, but man, I could go for a massage.

She shoots me a look. "And you know how a fairy godmother tastes?"

I realize how my comment came out, but I go with it. "Like all your dreams come true."

"You're telling me you've dated fairy godmothers?"

"Maybe I have."

"I've dated genies, then," she says, playing at one-up-manship as our waitress arrives. Natalie tells her what she wants, and I order the beef bibimbap for myself, so spicy it singes your hair off, then add in an appetizer and some beers.

We're here because Natalie loves spicy food. The hotter the better. In fact, she's challenged me to a few food dares over the last six months. Fortunately, I was born with fire-proof taste buds and a competitive will of iron, so I usually beat her, but I've got to hand it to the woman. She can down a habanero pepper like no one I've ever seen.

Not gonna lie. It was a massive turn-on watching her eat a couple of those bad boys on a burger one night a few weeks ago when we got some grub after work. There's just something about a woman who can handle her spice.

That is, it *would* have been a turn-on if I'd been thinking of her that way. And I hadn't, so I wasn't turned on.

Case closed.

A minute later, the waitress returns with two beers, and I raise a glass to toast Natalie. "To six months of your magic. You're better than a fairy godmother."

"To six months of solid employment, at last," she jokes. Natalie was bouncing around at various odd jobs before I hired her. She'd needed work, and she was blunt about it. In fact, the night she approached me in her job hunt perfectly underscores my point about dudes saying women are hot for us.

Because we have no clue if they actually are. We're all fumbling and bumbling around, blind to what women really want. Women are basically the most complicated creatures ever invented, and approximately twenty thousand times more complex than the world's smartest computer.

At my friend Spencer's wedding last fall to Natalie's sister Charlotte, Natalie made her way over to me with a determined look in her eyes, and I'd joked to my twin brother Nick, "She wants me."

Wrong. Dead-as-a-doornail wrong.

Turned out she was making a beeline for another reason. When we'd chatted the night before, I'd mentioned some of the issues my firm was facing—the main issue being my complete disorganization—and she'd devised a plan for how to improve operations and put my firm in a position to expand and win even bigger jobs. She'd presented it to me over a game of pool at the wedding hotel. Her proposal had been airtight and exactly what I soon realized I needed.

I'd hired her two weeks later.

Now, after half a year together, I can't imagine WH Carpentry & Construction without her running the business side of things. Her savvy frees me up to focus on what I'm good at—building, making, working.

She nudges my arm with her elbow. "Remember the day I started? And you went to an appointment that was actually on your schedule from a year before?"

I groan. "Don't remind me."

She shakes her head in amusement. "But I saved you! I called you literally as you arrived at the client's apartment building, about to go in and give an estimate on a kitchen you'd already redone."

I nod as the memory flashes before me. "Yup. Good with tools, bad with appointments."

"And now you're good with both," she says, her lips curved up in that winning smile of hers. I look away briefly. I can't stare at her smile. It would probably hypnotize me. Make me do its bidding.

"And business couldn't be better," I say. "We should be able to expand now, the way we first talked about. Hire more guys—regular employees, so we're not just relying on day laborers for each job."

"Exactly. With the new work we have lined up for the summer, we can bring some full-timers on, cover their health benefits, and all that good stuff." She rattles off some of the projects she'd booked—a number of high-end kitchen remodels. Since it's Manhattan, those gigs can net us six figures or more.

"By the way, I've been meaning to ask. How did you ever get to be so organized? Do you have file folders in your head? Admit it. It's like the Container Store up there," I say, tapping her noggin.

She pretends to pant, her tongue lolling out of her mouth like a dog in summer. "Don't get me excited. The Container Store is my favorite place in the universe, and I'm convinced I could happily live there."

"So that's the answer?" I ask as the waitress arrives with a fire chicken appetizer that's practically curling from the smoke. This one is going to be stomach scalding. Excellent. "Your affection for the store is how you became so organized?"

Natalie squares her shoulders. "Have I mentioned my clothes are hung by color in the closet? That all my books are arranged alphabetically, and that I never once missed a day of school in my life?"

"And your panties are probably arranged by—" I slam the brakes on the subject of her lingerie. Shit. Where is the fucking filter in my brain? I swear Floyd tampered with my head today. Maybe his hinges were faulty.

"By color," she answers with a chirpy little sound, like she knows I went there. She knows I slid into a zone where I shouldn't go.

But yet, here I am, asking more, "And the most popular shade is?"

An eyebrow rises, and the corner of her lips quirks up. It's like she just slid on the perfect flirty-girl face, and now I have one very ready-for-business appendage.

Fucking dicks. Sometimes it's unfair that we have these fuckers to do battle with all day. And believe me, it is an epic battle. Man versus hard-on.

Man rarely wins.

Boners are too powerful.

An answer falls from her glossy pink lips. Natalie wears some kind of sparkly pink gloss. Not lipstick. Yes, I know what gloss is. I've kissed plenty of women, and I'm not some Neanderthal with a toolbox who doesn't know the difference between gloss and lipstick. One is slick and tastes amazing coming off a girl's lips when I kiss her; the other one is thicker and tastes amazing coming off a girl's lips when I kiss her.

"White," she says, and the situation south of the border intensifies.

I grab a fork and dive into the fire chicken. Maybe that'll be the cure for wood. "And now I know where all your business skills come from. Underwear drawer organization."

"Pink's a popular one, too."

And we're talking steel right now. Pink panties on Miss All-American is pretty much a recipe for a Viagra Dick—constantly erect.

"Pink. White. As long as they're color-coded, that's what matters." She gestures to the chicken. "Time to blow our brains out."

We one-up each other in eating a chicken dish that tastes like a lit match going down your throat, then douse the flames with beer, and move on to the main course.

At the end of the meal, my phone buzzes twice.

Natalie points in the general direction of my pocket. "Work text," she says quickly, reminding me she set my phone to a double buzz when messages to the work number route to my personal phone.

As Natalie busies herself checking her own phone, I grab mine and open a message from Lila Mayweather.

I've got the go-ahead! Can't wait to discuss the new project with you. Would love to start soonest! When you come by tomorrow, can you bring along Natalie?

I smile. It kind of makes me proud that my clients love her so much. I'm about to show her the text, but she's still busy on her phone, tapping away. I can't help but wonder who she's texting. I'm tempted to peek, but I restrain myself. When she stops and puts her phone away, though, I catch a flash of one word—*torture*.

Interesting. But I'm not keen to play Sherlock tonight, so instead I show her Lila's text. "You're wanted, it seems."

She beams. "I wonder what it could be. Do you have any idea?"

I shake my head. "No clue. But we'll find out tomorrow. Think we can fit this in?"

"The next job doesn't start for a while. Let's get the details, but I think we can do it."

"Pretty sure you deserve a raise," I say.

She beams. "I'm really glad I've been able to help you, Wyatt."

"Me, too," I say, because even though she's a stone-cold fox, even though she's gorgeous in more ways than I can count, and even though if she weren't my assistant, I'd be a persistent motherfucker to get her to go home with me, she's also fucking amazing at what she does.

She sets down her napkin, looks at her watch, and shoots me a sad smile. "I should go. I have a class tonight. Only time I could get at the dojo this week."

"Totally understand," I say, and when she takes off, I half wonder if she's really going to class, or if some guy was texting her when she was checking out her phone. Maybe hanging out with me was torture? Nah. I'm a barrel of monkeys. Besides, I remind myself, it's not my place to know about her life beyond work.

That's exactly why I don't think of her when I head to my apartment later. Or when I take a shower. Or when I crash into bed, and thumb through an article of interesting facts about animals, including that dolphins never enter deep sleep. Their brains are too active.

That's one of the nice things about being me. I can turn off my brain.

Women are complicated, but the situation with Natalie is simple. I keep my hands to myself.

And I swear it's not made more complicated the next morning when Lila presents us with her plan.

CHAPTER THREE

Lila Mayweather serves us coffee in delicate china cups with a rose pattern around the edge. For the record, I'm not a delicate cup kind of guy. But when in Rome . . .

Seated in a high-backed chair in her dining room, Lila wears a tennis skirt, and her brown hair swings high in a well-groomed ponytail. Everything about her is impeccable, down to the fact that she offers us cream in one of those specialty thingamajigs with the spout and then holds up pewter tongs for sugar cubes.

"I'm all good," I say. I can't remember the last time I drank coffee from anything but a paper cup or a mug with a broken handle.

But Lila's home oozes class, and her remodel is one of the fanciest I've ever done. I have a feeling it's going to open a lot more doors for the business. She and Natalie had hit it off from the start, and right now they're discussing Natalie's martial arts skills.

Lila drops a hand on Natalie's arm, bare in her short-sleeved white blouse. "I'd love to take one of your classes sometime. I love to try new workouts."

"I promise I will make you sweat," Natalie says playfully, as she crosses her legs.

You can make me sweat.

What the fuck? The horny aliens are back, taking over my brain again.

"I've been wanting to learn self-defense. How long have you been teaching karate?"

Natalie is a high school karate champion. Yeah, like that's not a major turn-on. Not the high school part—the karate. But if I let myself linger on the fact that she knows how to fight, the flag will be flying at full mast all day long.

Instead, I think about sugar cubes. And rose petals on cups. And matching china. Because I'm not Floyd.

They chat for a few more minutes and I drain the coffee, because prissy cup or not, I'm a coffee whore, and I can pound that delicious substance morning, noon, or night. Lila sets down her mug, folds her hands in her lap, and says, "The reason I asked you both to be here today is I have an exciting new project. Craig is investing in some property, a beautiful new building, and I have carte blanche to redo the penthouse any way I see fit." Glee seems to radiate off the woman, as she shares more. "Naturally I thought of WH Carpentry & Construction first, and I'd love to see if you'd consider doing the kitchen remodel. I'm simply in love with what you've done here, and I can't imagine letting anyone else put his hands on my appliances."

I can't even try to contain my grin, not just because of the unexpected innuendo, but because the work could help fund the new hires. And the smile just stretches across my face because this would be the definition of a no-brainer. I'm not really sure why she wanted to set up coffee to ask me to do more work. Of course, I'm interested. I like work. I like building. I like happy clients.

"It sounds fantastic," I say.

"Where is this lovely new apartment?" Natalie asks.

"It's on the twenty-second floor. It's absolutely gorgeous, and it has a stunning view."

"Sounds amazing. What do you have in mind for a start date?"

"I thought first I could show it to you, so you know what you're working with," Lila suggests.

I nod. "Definitely. Want to check it out now?"

She laughs lightly and shakes her head. "Oh no, I'm sorry, I didn't make that clear. You'll need to take my private jet to get there."

I swallow dryly and look at Natalie. She blinks at me. Unspoken words pass between us. I'm pretty sure they are all of the *holy shit* variety.

You don't have to say *private jet* more than once for me to say *when do we take off?* So I do. I shrug happily. "When do we go wheels up?"

"Is the end of the week too soon? It's on the Strip. The building is near the Bellagio." She brings a hand to her chest. The egg-sized diamond on her finger nearly blinds me as she says contritely, "Oh my, I should have asked. Would you be willing to work in Las Vegas? I'd be happy to pay you twenty percent above your New York fees for the inconvenience of working out of town and needing to find the right crew and workers and so on."

I think this woman might be a fairy godmother.

"I would be thrilled to check it out, Lila," I say. "I'm sure we can figure out how to make it all possible."

Lila flashes me a smile then tips her forehead to Natalie. "That's why I thought of both of you. I know Natalie is vital to making all this happen," she says, waving a hand in the direction of the kitchen, "and it seemed to make sense for you to go together."

The last word echoes.

Together. Together. Together.

No one says a word at first, then the silence spreads. Grows heavier. Weightier.

I remind myself that we've had dinner just the two of us. What's the harm in traveling together?

I clear my throat and meet Natalie's blue-eyed gaze. I swear I see excitement in her eyes. "Natalie, would that work for you? For your schedule at the dojo?"

She nods at the speed of light. "Yes. And once we know the scope of the job, I'll do everything I can to make this fit into Wyatt's work."

Lila nearly bounces in her seat. "Wonderful. I can even arrange for you to stay in a suite at the Bellagio. Would those accommodations be suitable?"

She's serious. That's the most incredible part of her entire request. That she thinks there's a chance we'd find the Bellagio *unsuitable.* "Yes, I believe it would suit us just fine," I say, in a serious tone. "Natalie, does the Bellagio meet your standards?"

"Considering I'm operating at more of a Motel 6 level, I think the accommodations at the Bellagio would make me break out in cartwheels," she says to Lila, who laughs sweetly.

Cartwheels. Wouldn't mind seeing Natalie twirling upside-down. Preferably while wearing a short skirt.

"Do you need a room together or separate?" Lila asks, her eyes darting back and forth between us.

And it's almost as if we're puppies tumbling on top of each other, racing to answer *separate* in the same firm tone of voice. So there can be no confusion, we both repeat it: "Separate."

We chat some more, and when Lila excuses herself to make some calls, Natalie's phone dings with a text. As she reads it, her expression falls. "Crap. Hector can't make it in. Says he didn't get enough sleep last night."

Hector is the guy I was counting on to help me with the final details of the cabinet install today.

"Fuuuuuck," I say, like it has ten syllables. I heave a sigh. "This is why we need to hire some full-time people."

She nods. "We need some accountability. Regularity. He says he can be here tomorrow, though."

I shake my head. "Won't do. Besides, what if Sleeping Beauty doesn't get enough shut-eye again?"

She wraps her hand around my forearm. "Let me call around and see if I can round up any other last-minute guys."

Finishing a job on time is always my goal, and I can't let Lila down. "Don't worry about it. I'll do it all. I'll just stay late to finish."

Natalie shakes her finger at me. "You'll do no such thing. Working too many hours in a row is dangerous. I'll help you."

I give her a look. "Appreciate it, but Hector wasn't going to be doing schematics or scheduling. He uses a drill and a circular saw."

She arches an eyebrow then taps her chest. "Wait. After six months together, you think I can't operate a circular saw? Or hammer a nail?"

"I know you're capable enough to hammer a nail—"

She cuts me off and holds up three fingers. "I can fix a leaky faucet." Two fingers. "I can knock a grown man to the ground with my bare hands." Last finger. "And not only can I inhale habanero peppers, I can screw anything."

My jaw drops. I can't even respond. I can't even speak, and I don't think she's aware of the double entendre because she's focused on darting her hands to my waist, and holy fuck, that's a mighty nice spot for them. If she could move them just a bit lower, my fantasies might come true.

Fine, I've dreamed of screwing her hard. Like that's a fucking surprise.

She unfastens my tool belt, slings it around her waist, tightens the buckle, and proceeds to look *hot as fuck.*

Jeans. White blouse. My worn leather tool belt sitting low on her hips.

For the rest of the day I will be working next to her.

Please, please, please let the horny aliens inhabit the planet of another man's mind today.

* * *

Temptation, thy name is Natalie.

"Where'd you learn to play with tools like that?" I ask as we work side by side.

She rolls her eyes at me then sticks out her tongue. It doesn't have the intended effect. She looks cute. Just like when girls pull down their pants to moon you as some sort of insult. It's not an insult. It's a win. Not that any girls have done that lately. Come to think of it, no one's mooned me in years. Would be nice if Natalie broke my un-mooned streak.

"The same place you learned to play with dolls," she tosses back.

"Oh, shots fired," I say.

As she dips her hand into the tool belt for a screw, she says, "You think just because I'm a woman I'm not handy?"

I scoff. "That's the last thing you can pin on me, sweet-heart," I say, and then I stop. *Sweetheart*? I don't usually call her that. But, you know, it fits her.

She aligns the screw into the wood then says, "For your information, I learned from my mom."

"Your mom, the surgeon?"

"Yeah. Funny thing is, surgeons play with tools, too. Scalpels, scissors, even, get this"—she pauses, and her eyes glint with wicked playfulness—"drills."

I pretend to shudder. "Anyway, I'm impressed. I knew you could do the basics, but you've been keeping the extent of your handywoman skills a secret. Then again, you didn't tell me for months you were a ninja."

She laughs. "Not a ninja. Just a black belt, third level. And besides, I'm not trying to pretend I'm a master car-penter like you. I can get by, but I can't hammer like Wyatt Hammer. You're a master at hammering, right?"

I wiggle my eyebrows. "Like I had any other choice for a career." I grab a drill bit from the toolbox on the floor. "Anyway, you cool with going to Vegas?"

She nods. "Absolutely. I've never been. It sounds like fun," she says, then quickly adds, "I mean, not that we're going to sightsee. We have work to do."

"Hey, I'm sure we can find time to ride the rollercoaster or Ferris wheel or whatever you want. Play roulette, see a show. By the way, I meant it the other night when I said you deserve a raise. If this new job comes through, I'm giving you a ten percent pay increase." I line up the cabinet door. She's doing the same with the one next to me, when out of the corner of my eye I see the door start to slip.

On a fast track for her face.

In an instant, I'm behind her, my hands shooting out on each side of her, catching it before it swings wildly off the hinges.

"I got it," I say, gripping the cupboard door in place.

"Shit. That almost whacked—"

"Your head," I say softly.

She nods, her hair brushing against my cheek. That feels better than it should. Like, too good. "That would have sucked to have my face flattened by a cupboard," she says, trying to make light of it, but she takes a deep breath, and her shaky voice gives her away.

"But you're okay," I say, since now's not the time for jokes.

"Thanks to you. You moved fast."

"Didn't want anything to happen to you."

My chest is sealed to her back. My crotch presses against her rear. My face is in her neck, and as I breathe in, the scent of Natalie floods my brain. I've never been this close to her, and she smells exactly like I'd expect her to. Fresh. Clean. Like sunshine.

Like I'm lying in a hammock in the yard, the grass newly cut, and she wanders over as the golden light of late afternoon halos her face. She slips into the hammock, yanks off her shirt, tugs down my zipper, and we fuck. A lazy, unhurried afternoon screw, with this woman who smells like sunshine.

I inhale her one last time, and her breath catches.

She makes a little sound, a soft *oh*, and that sound does something to me. Makes me start thinking. Start wondering. Start tripping down the dangerous trail of *maybe Natalie's hot for me, too*. Maybe I'm not the only one nursing some lust. I swear I feel a shudder move through her body like a ripple in a lake.

"Be careful," I whisper, and I'm not sure if the directive is for her or me.

"I will."

"No face pancakes on the job, okay?" I say, and now I'm the one trying to make light of things.

I lower the cupboard door to the counter and back away. She turns around, looks down, sweeps a lock of hair from her forehead.

Neither one of us says anything more as we finish.

I reason if I can survive a day with her working beside me, I can handle a weekend trip.

What could possibly go wrong on a business trip to Vegas?

CHAPTER FOUR

I'm counting down the days till we leave, but I've got enough to keep me busy. Like seeing my little sister and brother on the way to my volunteer shift at the dog rescue the next morning.

"It's time to nix Elizabeth Lecter," I tell Josie as I bite into the seven-layer bar she gives me.

Josie's green eyes widen, and she slashes her hands through the air. "Does that mean you're done? Like totally done?" She takes a seat across from me at a lemon-yellow table at Sunshine Bakery. This is our mom's bakery, but Josie pretty much runs it now.

I point at the bar. "This shit is good," I tell her.

She hands one to Nick, my twin brother, and shrugs happily. "I know. I rock at baking."

"You might even be better than Mom," Nick says out of the corner of his mouth, as if he's whispering. "But don't tell her that."

Josie mimes zipping her lips, then points to my phone. The Facebook profile of one fake "Elizabeth Lecter" is on the screen. "You're really ready to get rid of our pretend friend Elizabeth? Even considering what she accomplished after Sunday night's episode?"

I slash a finger across my throat. "Time to kill her off, and all the others, too."

"Go out on a high note," Nick says, agreeing, as he rips off a chunk of the evidence of Josie's unparalleled talent in the kitchen.

"It won't ever get better than this. Look at that." I point at the phone. I grip my face and drop my jaw open, like Edward Munch's *The Scream*. "It's like my ex is melting from the pain."

Josie reads out loud the response my ex, Katrina, wrote earlier this week on her page: "Is nothing sacred? Does anyone know how much spoilers hurt? Might as well take a knife and rip it through my chest."

Nick mimes wiping tears from his eyes. "Wah, wah, wah."

I lean back in the chair and stretch my legs out in front of me. "This might have been our greatest accomplishment ever. I'm quite proud of our factory of fake Facebook profiles. But I've got to hand it to little Miss Elizabeth. She really owned it when it came to her *Game of Thrones* final episode spoiler."

Josie holds up one finger. "But let's not forget our made-up friend Emma Krueger's spoiler. Remember when she posted about the Hold the Door death? Katrina's tears were all over her wall that night." Josie high-fives me for that one.

"Only to be topped by Elinor Bates's epic message that Jon Snow was alive," I add, pride suffusing me at the memory of that greatest hit. "But even so, it's time to say good-bye. Our work is done."

Josie runs a hand through her pink-streaked hair. "Should we embrace a moment of silence before you kill them off?"

I affix a serious expression to my face, and the three of us bow our heads. A few seconds later, I look up and delete the profiles that rained sweet revenge on Katrina.

Elizabeth Lecter, Elinor Bates, and Emma Krueger are all made up, plucked from the names of Jane Austen heroines, Josie's nod to her literature degree, then paired with last names of some of the greatest movie villains of all time.

Some might wonder why I'd punk Katrina, a seemingly harmless ex-girlfriend who's also my former website designer. As in, *really* former. As in, I didn't date her while we were working together, I swear up and down. Sure, I'd thought she was cute, and she'd clearly felt the same about me, since she'd asked me out a couple of times while on the job. But I'd already learned my lesson *not* to get involved with someone connected to my business, even though the first time it had happened, with my college girlfriend, Roxy, she wasn't even properly connected to my business. She just *wanted* to be.

Anyway, once the website work was done, the log-in changed for better-safe-than-sorry reasons—thanks to my friend Chase's reminder to change passwords as often as you change underwear—Katrina and I had dated for half a year.

Now, allow me to explain how six pleasant months of dating could lead to this sort of fall-out. Mind you, during those six months no one cheated and we even enjoyed picnics in the goddamn park, and if there is one thing I'm not it's a picnic guy, but she liked them and I went along to make her happy. Alas, I didn't want more from Katrina, and I swear it had nothing to do with the picnic torture, so I'd ended things. *Amicably.* Like a nice guy.

Then Katrina went full mental nutcase on me and used her web skills to hack my company site and delete all my files.

Out of the blue.

Even after the passwords were changed.

Like a total lunatic.

Yeah, it was shitty. It cost me business. I'd even had to hire a lawyer to deal with the mess left behind. The problems it caused were among the reasons I'd needed help from someone to get organized again.

So I'd hit Katrina, an avowed hater of books and lover of all things *Game of Thrones*, right where it had hurt her the most. Josie and I had made up fake profiles of women who might potentially be clients for Katrina's web services, friended her on Facebook, and then posted spoilers every Sunday night on Katrina's wall, live and in real-time as each episode aired. Our prank only worked because Katrina's been on a job out of the country since the season started, and she can't find an Internet stream right away to watch her favorite show in the universe.

Boo-fucking-hoo.

It's pretty much the trolliest trolling ever, and one of the best-deserved paybacks, too. I mean, the chick fucked my business with an unlubricated Phillips-head screwdriver for no reason, which might, just might, be why I'm a tiny bit cautious of getting involved with anyone work-related.

But all good pranks come to an end, and it's time to say good-bye to this one. I close my Facebook app, then I clasp a hand over Josie's. "Mom and Dad would be proud you learned from the best. Right, bro?" I say to Nick, since the two of us are the kings of pranks, and we've passed on some of our top tips to Josie.

"It really is impressive what we've done with the brains they gave us," Nick says. "We use them for good, don't we?"

"Completely." I pop the rest of the seven-layer bar into my mouth, then stand up and brush one hand against the other. "We need to head to Little Friends to walk the dogs. Oh shit, that reminds me. Nick, can you handle the dogs on Friday? I've got to go to Vegas for a gig."

He raises an eyebrow. "You working in Vegas now?"

"I might be. A client is flying me out. It sounds like an awesome job. Really hoping it comes through."

"That's great. Good for you," Nick says with a pat on the back.

"Yeah, it should be a good trip."

I'm headed for the light orange door—the bakery is an homage to all things bright and cheery—when Josie says, "Funny."

I turn to face her. "What's funny?"

She shoots me a knowing look. "That you didn't mention Natalie is going along."

"Why is that funny?" I don't need to ask how she knows. Josie is Natalie's roommate, and they both live in Natalie's sister's old place. When Charlotte moved out and married Spencer, she rented her old pad to her sister, giving her a break on rent so Natalie could live in the city and teach night classes at a karate studio here. A few months ago, Josie's lease ran out so she moved in, too.

It's not weird for me that my little sister lives with her.

I swear it's not weird for me at all.

"I just find it odd that you didn't mention you were going with her," Josie remarks.

Nick shakes his head, laughing. "Dude, that's a recipe for trouble if I ever saw one."

"You should know," I fire back.

"That's why I said it."

I press my palms down against the air, the sign for *chill out*. "It's work, peeps."

Josie tightens the knot on her apron, a light blue number with cherries on it. "Either way, Natalie seems excited for the trip and to see Vegas for the first time."

My ears prick. "She does?" Fuck, my voice just rose at the end, like a ninth-grader rattling around in puberty. I shrug it off with a casual, "I mean, cool."

My bluff doesn't go unnoticed. Josie raises a knowing eyebrow but simply says, "Make sure she sees the sights, okay?"

"I will. Vegas sign. A gondola ride. Bellagio Fountains."

"What's underneath your zipper," Nick whispers in my ear, and I elbow the fucker.

"Just be a good guy. Like you always told me a girl deserves," Josie says as she returns to the counter, and her words tug at something inside me. At my heart's deepest wish—to be a good guy. Because I wasn't always. But if I am now, it's because of Josie. I fucking love that girl like nobody's business.

She points to both of us. "That applies to both of you as a general rule of thumb. I know exactly what the two of you are like. I grew up with you troublemakers, remember?"

I salute her and bring my heels together, standing at attention. "I'm always a good guy, Josie."

Nick and I leave, heading for Little Friends dog rescue where we volunteer.

"Do you even know how to be a good boy?" he asks as we walk up Columbus, the warm spring air surrounding us.

I grab my shades from my T-shirt neckline and drop them over my eyes. "Yes. I do the opposite from you."

"You are going to be so fucked," he says, shaking his head as he laughs at me. We sidestep a jogger in neon pink leggings while cabs and cars chug along on the avenue. "You've had it bad for Natalie since Spencer's wedding. Remember?"

I wave a hand dismissively. "Nah, that's not true."

"Dude, you told me she wanted you when she came over to dance with me at the wedding."

"She did want me."

"My point exactly. You only say that when you want a girl."

I stare up at the blue sky. "Pretty sure I say that all the time. I'm a cocky bastard, right?" I wink, then clap him on the shoulder as we reach the crosswalk. "Relax, cowboy. Even if I once wanted her, I'm a master at self-control."

He scoffs. "Self-control. Words never used before to describe my little brother."

I pretend to laugh. "Maybe you don't know me that well."

"I think I know you better than anyone."

"Then, tell me this, oh wise one—how else would I have managed the feat of the century in staying away from her for all these months?" I arch a challenging eyebrow at Nick, waiting for him to give it back to me.

He pushes his glasses higher and nods slightly. "Fine, fine. You have some self-control." He shakes his head like he doesn't believe it.

But I believe it.

I have to.

Especially when three days later, I get on a private jet with Natalie Rhodes, temptation made flesh, the All-American black belt with a tongue of iron fire.

As she settles down into a beige leather seat and crosses her legs, she shoots me a smile.

That sweet, sexy smile.

Fuck, being a good boy is way overrated. I want to be bad with her.

CHAPTER FIVE

I could get used to this. The leather seats that recline all the way. The impeccable service, including a three-course lunch. A quiet ride in the lap of luxury next to Natalie.

Lila snoozes in her seat across the aisle. She popped a Xanax. Flying makes her anxious, she'd said, so she's in the land of nod, a black satin eye mask snug on her face.

"Can I get you anything else?" the flight attendant asks us.

I do a double take. For a split second, it registers that she's pretty. She's been serving us the whole flight, but it just hit me—her looks. Silky red hair, full lips, and warm brown eyes, along with a tight, trim figure. But then, all thoughts of her fall out of my head. And that's not just because it would be rude to hit on the flight attendant on Lila's plane, and it would also be classless to hit on her in front of an employee. But the reality is I don't really want to get to know *her* more. I'm kind of interested in talking to Natalie on this flight. Even though we tease each other at the office, and even though we've gone to dinner a few times, we mostly chat about work. There's a lot I don't know about her.

The attendant clears our Ahi tuna lunch dishes and asks if we'd like to watch a movie. I shift my focus to Natalie, letting her decide. She shakes her head and says, "I think I'll read."

But she doesn't read. She doesn't break out her Kindle or a paperback. Instead, she nudges me with her elbow and says, "I never imagined working for a construction firm meant I'd fly to Vegas like this. I should have tracked you down long ago. I would never have taken on all the crummy jobs I had before."

I laugh. "Tell me more about your checkered work history." I don't actually know a lot about what she did prior to working for me. Her résumé didn't score her the gig. Her gumption did.

She arches an eyebrow. "Like the time I worked for a phone sex operation?"

My eyes nearly pop out of my head. Then I school my expression and do my damnedest to act unfazed. "Oh, yeah?"

She nods. "It was kinda awesome. We did it all, but we specialized in furries and feet."

I do my best to maintain a straight face as sights and sounds of Natalie twirling a phone cord as she purrs huskily about the high heels on her tiny feet, flash like a neon billboard before my eyes. I swallow then manage a dry, "Really?"

I'm not sure if I'm turned on or wigged out. Maybe both. Mostly turned on, though.

She nods several times. "You have no idea how many men have foot fetishes until you do phone sex. They want to hear you walking around in your heels. They like the sound they make on a hard wood—pun intended—floor."

Damn, I love puns. I'm motherfucking crazy about them. But I've got no clue how to react to that one. I scrub a hand across my jaw. This is a whole new side to Natalie. And I can't help but picture her strutting across the floor in stilettos. She's already an intoxicating combo of cheerleader looks and tomboy heart—add in heels, and I'd be a goner. For the record, I'm not a foot fetishist whatsoever, but I bet she'd look sinfully sexy in four-inch pumps. Red ones. With her legs wrapped around my waist as I fuck her against the wall.

"And furries?" I ask, doing my best to stay rooted in the bizarre fetish portion of the convo, not the filthy personal fantasy part.

"People who wear full fur-suit costumes," she explains.

"I *get* what that is." I frown in confusion. "What I don't get is that furries seem to be more of a real life thing."

She nods exaggeratedly. "Oh, it's *huge* in phone sex. You pretend to be wearing a full fox suit. Or sometimes a squirrel outfit. Raccoons were also popular. But mostly a sexy squirrel. That was the favorite."

I'm trying. I swear I'm trying. But picturing Natalie whispering dirty words like *rub your furry tail against me as I store nuts in my cheeks* doesn't compute. "Men called in wanting to get it on with a gal in a squirrel suit?"

She nods. "It's called yiffing. Crazy, huh?"

I run a hand through my thick hair, a little wavy today. "A bit, but whatever floats your boat."

She arches an eyebrow. "Admit it. You're shocked."

"Nah," I say, acting all cool. Then I think *fuck it.* "Okay fine. Maybe a little."

A huge smile flashes on her face. "Gotcha." She points at me, and victory sparkles in her light blue eyes.

"Got me at what?"

"I heard you like pranks. Josie told me."

I crack up and shake my head in appreciation. "Well done," I say, then slowly clap. "You win at pulling my leg."

I straighten out my left leg, and she does her best charade to yank it. I pretend she captured it, and she tugs harder at the air, my leg like a big fish she's captured.

She grunts as she reels it in, then I set my foot down on the ground and knock fists with her. "Seriously. Dinner is on me tonight."

"It better always be on you," she says, then adds for emphasis, "*Boss.*"

Ah, there's that reminder.

"Anyway," she continues, "I might have been pulling your leg. But everything I said is true. I never said *I* made the calls. And I do know all that because I did work for a phone sex company. I just wasn't an operator myself. I screened the girls who wanted to work for us, set up the schedules, made sure they were paid, logged all the calls. It was weirdly fun."

"And I'm weirdly impressed." I would never have pegged the phone sex business as part of Natalie's work history, but the way she describes it completely fits her organizational skills.

She punches my bicep playfully. "And I wasn't technically lying."

"You were technically entertaining the hell out of me, though."

"Good," she says with a bright smile. "Want to know about more of my past jobs? I've had some interesting ones."

"Sure," I say, stretching out my long legs and thoroughly enjoying the legroom, not to mention the conversation.

"After the phone sex company I worked as a pet pedicurist."

"That's a job?"

She nods, the look in her eyes intense. "Hell, yeah. And it's not a bad way to make a living. You have no idea what wealthy Manhattanites will pay to have someone come to their home and clip the chihuahua's claws."

"Why not stick with it then?"

"Shockingly, I didn't want to spend my entire life working on dog feet. Don't get me wrong. I love dogs, and paws are awesome, but when it started conflicting with my schedule at the dojo in the evenings I had to let it go."

I tap her knee. "Which brings us to your true passion. Administering a side-kick to the head."

She pretends to punch me in the chest, coming *this* close. "Or the heart."

Her eyes glint. For a flash, I see something in them. Or maybe it's just that her words feel like a warning, like she really could deliver a blow to my heart.

I blink then look away.

She lowers her arm, placing her hands in her lap. "I do love it, though." Her tone is calmer now, more serious than when she riffed on yiffing and feet, on paws and claws. "Always have."

"Since you were little?"

"My parents sent me to karate class when I was six. I had a lot of energy, and it was a great place for me to burn it off. I grew to love it. The techniques, the skills, and most of all, the fact that you can always improve." She raises her eyes, meeting mine. In this moment, she seems to be shedding a layer that was between us—the boss-assistant one, maybe—as she ventures into more personal territory. "I also really love teaching it. My favorite is the self-defense part. I really want to keep teaching women self-defense and using martial arts for that. I feel like it's this one special thing I can do, you know?"

Her voice is vulnerable, like she wants reassurance that her admission means something to me. That I'll treat it with care. And I will. "I completely know what you mean, and I suspect you're fantastic at it."

"Don't get me wrong. I love working for your company, too, and my job at WH is a fantastic one," she says. Then a soft smile curves her lips, spreading until it turns into a yawn. A huge open-jawed yawn. She brings her hand to her mouth. "I think I hear a nap calling my name."

A few minutes later, she's sound asleep in her seat. A little after that, her head slides to my shoulder. Then, when she's deep in REM, her upper body slouches down, down, down . . . her head hitting my lap.

And that's how I spend the rest of the flight with Natalie curled in my lap.

Yes, it turns me on. Yes, I'm fucking aroused. And yes, my mind is filled with a reel of images of where her head could be if she woke up, shifted a few inches, and opened her mouth wide.

I inch back in the seat, trying to give Natalie's face some distance from the family jewels.

Soon enough, we begin the descent into Las Vegas. She wakes as we land and shoots straight up, her eyes darting all around as if she's registering where she is as she comes to. "Did I . . .?"

She points at my legs.

"Sleep on my lap?"

She nods.

"Yes."

Her eyes widen to saucer size. "Did I do that?" She points frantically at my crotch.

Ah, fuck. She noticed the banana in my pocket. I cycle through a litany of potential excuses for sporting wood during her afternoon lap nap when my eyes follow her finger. It's not my dick she's pointing at. It's the wet spot on my jeans. The huge wet spot that could only be caused by—

She brings a hand to her chest. "I'm so sorry I drooled on you."

I crack up. "Sweetheart, you can drool on me anytime."

She flashes an apologetic smile, then reaches into her back pocket for her phone, presumably. When she comes up empty, I peer around, spotting it on the floor by my feet, where it must have fallen while she slept.

I reach down to grab it for her, and I do my best to look away, but I can't help but notice the end of a message from her sister that appears on the screen.

I knew you'd feel this way!

What way, I wonder?

CHAPTER SIX

The Eiffel Tower is a dwarf. The Ferris wheel spins like a miniature toy, and the rollercoaster of New York-New York wraps around that casino like an architect's model. Up here, on the twenty-second floor of Lila's husband's new palace, we are kings and queens of a city of royals.

This building is one of the tallest in town. Surely it'll be a home for billboards soon enough, as high as the entire tower, beckoning tourists to glittery extravaganzas for the senses. For now, it's potentially the site of my next job.

I'm still not entirely sure why Lila wants me rather than someone local, so I ask her. I've built a reputation on honesty—no need to change that now. She's next to me, her arms crossed, a look of pride in her eyes as she gazes at the expansive view of the city of sin from the floor-to-ceiling windows in her living room.

"Do you like it? The place is lovely but the kitchen is a mess, isn't it?" Lila waves her arm toward the red stove, the black cabinetry, and the emerald green countertop. "Can you turn it around?"

"Absolutely. We'll tie everything together, and make it the centerpiece of the home you want. But I've got to ask, Mrs. Mayweather—why not find someone local? Any contractor would be glad to work in this gorgeous space."

"Absolutely. We'll modernize everything, and make it the centerpiece of the home you want. But I've got to ask, Mrs. Mayweather—why not find someone local? Any contractor would be glad to work in this gorgeous space."

She turns to me, meets my eyes, and laughs politely. "You're sweet to say that. But do you know how hard it is to find someone you trust? To let them into your home? Especially in a new city?" Her pitch rises, and she fidgets with her strand of pearls. From her unsaid words, I get the feeling Lila has encountered some bad apples previously. "There are so many predatory contractors disguised as your friend."

I almost want to knock fists in solidarity, because do I ever know bad apples. My college girlfriend, Roxy, was the rottenest one of all, but I'd have never known it at the time. After graduation, she encouraged me to start a handyman business, became my biggest cheerleader, and helped brainstorm a business plan. When she walked away for some dude on Wall Street making bigger bank, she did everything she possibly could on her way out the door to tear off a chunk of WH Carpentry & Construction with her bare teeth and keep it for herself. She was like a koala bear who turned out to be an alligator.

I nod at Lila, since I don't care for bad apples, alligators, or ex-girlfriends who hide their crazy far too well. "I hear ya. I appreciate you saying you can trust me, and I'm glad you feel that way. Means a lot."

"Plus, you finished on time, and in Manhattan none of my friends have found a single contractor who does." She slashes her hand through the air and raises her chin, as if she's offended by the indignities her friends have suffered in this regard. "You're a rare breed, Wyatt, and the thing I need most is to finish on time, since I want to have this place ready to host a gala for one of my favorite charities. A local philanthropist, Sophie Winston, is going to help me set it up. Will it be too hard to manage the work from afar?"

I turn around and drink in the layout once more. It's an open floor plan with copious space, a sunken living room, and gorgeous bedrooms. The style is modern and clean. White walls, simple furniture, and light hardwood floors. The kitchen, by contrast, is a mismatched mess, like a drunk monkey designed it while noshing on a spiked banana.

Natalie strides out of the kitchen where she's been taking measurements. She exits purposefully, her closed laptop in her hands, scribbling on a notepad on top of the computer.

"Hey, Natalie," I call out. "Think we can manage this job? We'll need an electrician, and we'll need to find some local suppliers for parts."

"Actually," Lila says, holding up a finger to chime in, "you won't even have to do that. You can use all your regular suppliers in New York and fly everything out on my plane."

I rein in a grin. Jesus fucking Christ. She is a fairy godmother. She's trying to make all my work dreams come true.

Natalie stands next to me. "And when it comes to an electrician, I already have one. I talked to a friend who runs Edge, a nightclub here. He'll hook us up with his guy for the electrical, as well as anyone we need for other specialized jobs. You'd just need to be here to do the labor," Natalie says to me, then she turns to Lila. "We can do it. I can manage it all remotely, and Wyatt can be on-site to do the work. We'll make it happen."

"Wonderful! I'm so thrilled," Lila says, her grin as wide as the Strip. "This benefit is so important to me, and I want my home to shine. Do you have a sense if you can meet the budget?" she asks, then tells me what she's willing to spend. The number has many zeros and nearly unhinges my jaw.

"I don't think that should be a problem. Why don't we go work on an estimate, send it to you, and then—"

Lila jumps in. "And then I can sign off on it tonight!"

Bibbidi-bobbidi-boo indeed.

Once inside the elevator, it's just Natalie and me while Lila stays behind. The doors close with a soft *whoosh,* and I turn to my assistant. "Can I just say it now?"

"The part where you're giving me a twenty percent raise?" she asks playfully.

I laugh. "Pretty sure I said ten percent."

"Ten percent. Twenty percent. What's the difference?"

The car descends softly. "Seriously, though. I will need to pay you extra for this. It's a ton of work."

"Twist my arm," she says and hands me her arm.

I pretend to torque it into a corkscrew.

"Ouch, ouch, ouch," she says, contorting her face.

I let go. "But officially, the answer is yes. The raise starts today. Thanks to Lila."

"Even though she hasn't officially signed off?"

I wave a hand in the air. "It's as good as a done deal."

I offer her a hand to shake, and instead she throws her arms around me. "Thank you so much," she says in the most heartfelt tone, her lips near my neck, her breasts snug to my chest, her fingers close to my hair.

"You're worth it," I say.

And you smell fucking amazing. And you feel spectacular. And I am a motherfucking master of self-control because all I want to do is hit the stop button, hitch your leg around my hip, and screw you hard.

"I can do my videos now." She pumps her fist in victory as we separate.

"Videos?"

Her entire face is animated. Her eyes are lit like sparklers. "I just started working on a series of self-defense videos. Like the kind you see on YouTube. I want them to be well-produced, and I think if they are, I can attract new students to my classes."

I smile. "Never knew that. That's fantastic. Are you shooting them yet, or still in the planning process?"

"I've made a few, but I need them to be a better quality. They're missing a certain something. I think I know what it is, but I didn't have the funds to keep making them at the level I need," she says quickly, then her tone switches, as if she's apologizing for her hopefulness. "It probably sounds silly—my self-defense dreams." She gives a dismissive wave.

I grab her arm. "No. It doesn't sound silly in the least. Dreams never are. Now you can go after them the way you want."

She shoots me that smile that always disarms me, that hooks into my heart and threatens to wreak havoc with my life. It's such an honest smile; it says she's this totally straightforward person who lays it all out up front. Who doles out compliments, who shares in excitement, who doesn't hide who she is or what she wants. All of that from the curve of her lips, the way her blue eyes light up, how her entire face glows . . . Fuck, I'm getting lost in this one part of her, and I've got to get it together. To remember the alligators . . . the crazy alligators, even though I can't possibly put Natalie in that reptilian category.

Still, once bitten, twice shy, so it's time to let these thoughts of her go. I start by releasing her arm.

As we reach the ground floor and exit into the lobby, she says, "I have to admit, I'll kind of miss seeing you around the office when you're out here for a few weeks working on Lila's home."

And hell, if that comment doesn't hook into me even more. Before I can show off my mastery of self-control, the unfiltered portion of my brain wrests control. "And you know what? I'll miss you, too," I say, and it's not the horny aliens. It's just me.

We reach the revolving door and head into the Vegas afternoon sun for the quick walk to the Bellagio.

Natalie points in the direction we came. "I think I cut you off earlier. When we first stepped into the elevator and you said *can I just say it?*"

I laugh as she rewinds us back to what I'd been thinking as we left the penthouse. "Just . . . *holy shit*. Lila is the most generous person I've ever met."

"She is generous. But you heard what she said. You've earned the right to her generosity." There's no teasing now in Natalie's tone, and her compliment reminds me what matters—being a good guy. At work. In life. With women.

I need to stop thinking of banging Natalie in elevators, and, on that same note, of missing her. That's girlfriend-level stuff. Natalie is just an employee. Nothing more.

I look at my watch. "It's nearly four. Think there's any chance we can find a watering hole willing to serve us at this early hour?" I joke, since it's Vegas and round-the-clock drinking is not only possible but encouraged.

"Absolutely. Let's grab something at the Bellagio."

"Sounds good. How about an early dinner, some drinks, and an estimate?" See? I'm all work.

"And then maybe we can celebrate later and ride the rollercoaster?"

I say yes, because all work and no play makes Wyatt a dull boy.

CHAPTER SEVEN

Five hours later, Natalie shows me exactly where she wants to land a knifehand strike to my throat.

"And then just to make sure you're down, I'd spin around like this," she says quickly, and executes a fast, low kick in the vicinity of my knee. "But, I'd totally kick you harder, and you'd crash to the ground." She winks. "That was just my bar kick."

I shudder. "I'd hate to run into you in a dark alley, Sensei Natalie, whether you're bringing your bar kick or your karate chop to my neck."

We're at a noisy bar with rock music at the New York-New York hotel, since the rollercoaster is here. Natalie is already two drinks in—mojitos are her choice tonight. She's been detailing exactly what she wants to do in her self-defense videos. Most of the time, she demonstrates the moves on me. Well, not like full demo where I'm flat on my ass, but she's been pretending to punch me.

Maybe I'm a masochist, but I love it. Or maybe I'm simply an attention hog for this woman. Whatever the reason, the outcome is all good in my book—her hands on me. But then, everything is good right now, because the job is a big green go, and we are celebrating.

We worked up an estimate when we returned to the Bellagio. Natalie emailed it to Lila. Thirty minutes later, Lila wrote back with: "*Wonderful! The first check will be deposited on Monday.*"

Which means a raise for Natalie, and the path to expansion for me. It also means Natalie's racing along the highway to buzzed, and I'm not too far behind her. She's changed from her work clothes. She wears a red skirt with some kind of surreal flower pattern, black heels, and a silky black top. The heels are hot, but flip-flops would have fit the bill, too.

See, I'm an everything guy. I don't have a particular type when it comes to women. Some gentlemen prefer blondes, some dig redheads, and some go bananas for women with exotic looks. Me? I'm an omnivore when it comes to the ladies, and I have a big, hearty appetite.

Right now, though, with Natalie radiating energy and excitement, I'm thinking blonde with a side of spanking is my favorite. Maybe an appetizer of hot hungry kisses, a main dish of hardcore fucking, and for dessert, we'd go for doubles.

Shit.

I went there again.

I blink away the not-safe-for-work thoughts and try to come up with a generic topic to riff on to get my mind back into the good-guy zone. Something that won't set my fantasies on fire. Maybe what invoices we need to file. Or new tools to order. Possibly even what's next on the schedule after this new Vegas job.

But I'm not in the mood to discuss work, so I flash onto something I read earlier in the week. As I'm about to tell her my favorite weird fact I learned recently—cats don't have collarbones like we do, which explains why they can squeeze into tiny openings the size of their heads—she moves in close to me as Bon Jovi plays on the sound system.

"Look over there," she says in a bare whisper. "She's telling him all her furry fantasies."

I follow her gaze to a couple across the bar. The dude is Brooks Brothers all the way from the navy suit to the loosened red tie. The woman appears to be a colleague, judging from the crisp white blouse, or maybe she's someone he just closed a business deal with. But with his arm draped over her shoulder, it sure looks as if he's going to close some other kind of deal.

"His raccoon suit is up in his room," I say, since Natalie's game sounds like more fun than cat facts. I tip my forehead to a Goth-looking woman with earplugs and the tattooed guy next to her, knocking back shots. "She dresses up like Little Bo Peep so he can spank her with a . . . fuck, what are they called?"

She rolls her eyes. "Wyatt," she says, in a faux admonishing tone, "they're called crooks."

I snap my fingers. "That's it. He smacks her ass with a crook."

For a flash of a second, Natalie's breath seems to rush from her lips. "Kinda sounds like fun," she says in a saucy tone, like maybe she'd want to play that sort of game. "What if I lost my sheep?"

And evidently, she does.

"Want me to help you find them?"

The look in her eyes is inviting. "Yes. But to find them I need another drink. I want a vodka tonic this time," she says, and since the bartender is circling, I order two.

As he sets to work pouring, she parks her chin in her hand, looking straight at me. "I love vodka tonic. Want to know why?"

"You bet I do."

But before she can reveal the root of her love for this liquor, the phone dings from her purse, bleating loudly enough to get our attention. She fishes around for it and clutches it close to her chest like a precious thing. "It's Lila. At this rate, she's probably calling to say she wants to pay us even more."

"Fuck, yeah. And I'll give *you* all the extra." I puff out my chest. "Because I'm a generous guy."

See? I can treat her well, and I'm not even thinking of nailing her.

This second, that is. Ten seconds ago I totally was.

"I think I might love you," she says, and blows me a kiss as the bartender delivers our round.

She slides open the screen, and her expression transforms. Her lips curve down, and she lets out a long, never-ending "oh fuck."

Her eyes slip shut, and she swallows then takes a breath. "Fuck a duck," she says, but it doesn't sound cute or playful. She sounds frustrated.

My heart pounds against my rib cage, and worry takes root. "What is it, Natalie?" I ask, reaching for her arm.

She opens her eyes and speaks in a monotone. "The job is cancelled."

All the buzz leaks out of me. "For real?"

That just doesn't compute.

She nods.

"Are you kidding me?" I ask again, because this makes zero sense.

"I wish," she says flatly, then reads the screen aloud. "*Dear Natalie: I'm so sorry to be sending this, but Mr. Mayweather had a deal on another property that just went south. Sadly, I have to put the Vegas remodel on hold. I'm hopeful to return to it soon, and please know I can't wait to work with WH Carpentry & Construction on it.*

P.S. I'm taking the jet home right now to comfort him. I know it's not nearly the same, but I've arranged for first-class tickets on a commercial airline for you and Wyatt, leaving tomorrow afternoon. The tickets are in your email. I hope the service is sufficient. My best, and we will regroup soon."

Natalie drops the phone on the bar with a dejected clang, the sound resonating in my bones.

Because . . .

Fuck a motherfucking flock of ducks. This stings.

I grab the vodka tonic and down half in one big gulp. She does the same with hers.

"I'm sad, Wyatt," she says, as those pretty lips droop once more.

And that does it for me. I can't stand the thought of this girl being sad. I want that smile back on her face, and I'm going to find a way to do it. I don't care about how this job loss makes *me* feel. I need to make Natalie happy again, and that will also take my mind off this shitty news. "Hey," I say, gripping her shoulder. "We're in Vegas. Let's make the best of it. Okay?"

She sighs dejectedly.

I park my hands on both her shoulders. "Seriously. We'll figure this out. We'll make this work. I'll give you the raise regardless. But right now, right here, we have fun. Got it?"

She shakes her head. "You're sweet to say that, but you don't have to give me the raise. I know it was conditional on the Mayweather job."

"No," I say, correcting her, holding her gaze. "It was conditional on you being amazing at what you do. And that hasn't changed. We're not going to let one setback get us down. You've never been to Vegas before, and I promised to show you the sights. You name it. This town is yours, and we're doing whatever you want tonight."

She shrugs then waves a hand dismissively. "I should have known better. It was a ridiculous, overpaying, crazy job. It was too good to be true. There's no such thing as calorie-free chocolate, or a guy who's funny, well hung, and sweet." I want to protest, but she's right, since no way am I sweet, "And the same is true for a client willing to pay twenty percent more for this job. They're all unicorns."

"Natalie, it's not ridiculous. It's reasonable. You said it earlier. We're good at what we do. Lila knows that. This is just a snag. Deals fall apart. I've seen this happen time and time again in this business. Hell, Nick goes through this with his job. I'm sure your sister would say the same. I bet she and Spencer have had deals from suppliers that fell through—it's just the way it goes. We wanted it, it didn't happen, we move on." Since she hasn't agreed to my make-the-most-of-the-night proposition yet, I keep going, the determined mofo in me steering the ship. "And no matter what, you still get a raise, so you can make your videos. And tonight? We're having the time of our life. Deal?"

Her lips twitch, and that's the hint I need to press on more. I won't give her a chance to be bummed. I search the bar quickly, and my eyes land on a middle-aged man in a turquoise tropical shirt, and a woman wearing a matching one. I drop my hand from Natalie's shoulder, but lean in close and whisper, "Handcuffs for the Hawaiian shirt duo. Tonight, he's cuffing her. And he's giving it to her good and hard against a bedpost in the Flamingo."

"Yes," she whispers conspiratorially, picking up the thread, like she can't resist this game. "They've been married for twenty years, and they still do it every night."

That's an interesting addition. I arch an eyebrow. "That sound like something you'd like, sweetheart?"

She nods. "Someday. Especially since my last boyfriend wasn't like—" She cuts herself off. "I shouldn't say it."

My curiosity is piqued. "No, you *should* say it. I want to know."

She grabs her glass and takes another sip.

"Tell me, Natalie. He wasn't *like what*?"

She runs her fingertip along the rim of the glass, avoiding answering.

I give her a pointed look. "Fess up. He didn't want to cuff you? Spank you with a crook? Do it every night?"

Because I'd cuff her. I'd tie her up. I'd spank her. I'd fuck her on all fours. In a car. On a plane. Anywhere and everywhere and every night. No hang-ups for this guy.

"Fine. He wasn't very . . . *interesting* in bed."

And I'm hard. Just like that. Not because of her ex, but because of what this implies—that she is *interesting* in bed, and I'm very interested in interesting things happening between the sheets with her.

"And you prefer interesting, I take it?"

"Strange, that I," she says with a wiggle of her eyebrows, "at the least, prefer regular nookie. And I think handcuffs, doggie style, public sex, and spanking are just fine and dandy." She clasps a hand to her mouth and cringes. "Shit. I didn't say that out loud, did I?"

"Every single delicious word." I smirk. "So, we have a deal? No more sad Natalie tonight?"

She exhales, nibbles on the corner of her lips, then grins playfully. "As long as I can ride the rollercoaster, it's a deal."

"You'll get your rollercoaster, and you'll get the full Vegas experience. Nothing less," I say, holding out my hand.

She takes it and we shake. "Full Vegas experience."

"One night. We're going to fit it all in."

"We'll go all out." She sweeps her arm grandly.

"Let loose."

"Throw caution to the wind," she says with a full-wattage grin. She reaches for her vodka tonic, her elbow knocking her phone closer to me. Out of the corner of my eye, I see her text messages. The one from Lila is the most recent. But beneath it is one to Charlotte she must have opened after closing the Lila one, and the words flash temptation at me, like a line I shouldn't cross but will anyway.

I want him so badly.

And that's all I need to know. The words embolden me, and I return to what I'm pretty sure she was hinting at before Lila's message landed. I tap her glass. "Tell me, why do you like vodka tonics?"

"Guess," she says, inching close, her command a flirty invitation.

"Because of how it tastes on your lips when I kiss you?" I ask, trying that on for size.

She says one word. *Yes.*

And before I know it, I'm kissing Natalie.

CHAPTER EIGHT

Let's back up.

How did we get from not kissing to kissing? What was that turning point? Did she lean into me? Did I move closer to her? Details matter. I'll gladly share them.

Start with six months of sexual tension. Add in two mojitos for her, two beers for me, and a couple vodka tonics. Stir that with some bad news on the business front, and top it with the cherry of Natalie's hit-me-over-the-head-with-a-stick comment that left no question as to what she wanted . . . and here I am.

We don't lean into each other. There's no inch-by-slow-sensual-inch pull. It's not a slow burn.

It's a fiery crash. We're two cars speeding on the highway of this night, and we slam into each other, crawl across the hoods, and kiss like crazy.

Nothing is tentative about this. We go from not kissing to kissing in less than sixty nanoseconds. Yeah, I don't really know what a nanosecond is, either. But it happens in no time.

And now my hand is in her hair, yanking her close as we crush our lips together. We kiss hard and rough, fueled by pent-up desire and more than enough vodka and rum to make this inevitable.

Her teeth scrape me, and I growl, loving her roughness. I suck hard on her bottom lip, and I'm rewarded by nearly the same sound from her. She's like a tiger, and together we're animals.

I grip her head tighter, and her hands are all over me— in my hair, then down my chest, then along my arms. We kiss so deeply, it's like we're trying to climb each other.

At some point, she breaks off, breathes out hard, then whispers in my ear, "I've wanted to do that for so long."

"Not as long as I have. Now get those lips back on mine," I tell her, and she complies.

My hands cup her cheeks, but I'm not gentle, and she doesn't want me that way. She's not a gentle girl. She's badass and tough, and she wants what I want. I hold her face tightly in my hands, and she practically crawls into my lap in a rush to get closer, then closer still as she presses her tits against my chest.

I'm seated on a stool at the bar, and we are putting on some kind of show. But I don't care.

My tongue searches and hunts, wanting to taste every corner of her mouth, savoring the vodka and the tonic and, most of all, the *Natalie*. She whimpers and moans, and I swallow every sexy sound she makes.

This stool is ours. This bar is ours. The night belongs to this kiss, because it's not a starter kiss. It contains all the clues necessary to assemble the puzzle of where this night will end.

With unwavering certainty, I know what kind of kiss this is.

As I explore her mouth, and she claims mine with equal urgency, I know that I will be fucking Natalie tonight.

* * *

Somehow we make it out of the bar. I pay the bill, she grabs her purse and phone, and we stumble into the big maw of New York-New York.

"So, this whole Vegas experience." Her eyes are flirty, her voice is naughty, and her hips sway as she walks. "Does the rollercoaster *come* next?"

Now that's an invitation if I've ever heard one. I RSVP to it. "Let's ride it now. We're making the most of every single second in this town."

I don't say the next part—that come Monday we go back to normal. To work. Anything more than tonight is too risky, but I don't want to lay down ground rules now. I want to be in the moment tonight. Besides, the vodka is already telling my brain *who gives a crap about Monday?* "We do it all," I say instead, because that makes a helluva lot more sense right now than thinking about consequences.

"Good." She grabs the neckline of my black T-shirt as we stop in front of Nathan's Famous Hot Dogs, where patrons stuff foot-longs and cheesesteaks in their mouths. "Because I love rollercoasters," she says, grinding against me in the bright light of the casino hallway, the *plink-plink-plink* of nearby slot machine payoffs and the spinning of roulette wheels gliding through the air.

I grasp her hips in my hands so she can feel the hard length of me against her. She gasps as she comes in contact with my hard-on, then a sweet, sexy moan slips from her lips. Her reaction is priceless and perfect. "How much do you love rollercoasters?" I ask.

"Just you wait 'til you hear me scream on the drop. Then you'll know how much."

I raise an eyebrow. "Sweetheart, I'm going to take you for a helluva ride."

Somehow, we pull apart.

We walk and we kiss. We follow the signs for the ride, and stop to make out on the way. I press her to the wall and kiss her neck, my stubble dragging against her soft skin. She moans when I do that, and her sounds drive me crazy. I want to hear all her murmurs and sexy cries, be the reason she makes them, and then make her groan and moan again.

We manage to traverse another hundred feet or so, then up the escalator where the entrance to the joint arcade and rollercoaster looms near.

But I need to touch her again, so I spin her around, back her up to the wall, and pin her wrists at her sides, pressing my body to hers and crushing her lips once more with mine. When I manage to pull away, I drag my mouth to her earlobe, and bite. She lets out a soft yelp. "Want you so much," I tell her.

"God, you have no idea. Being near you is torture. I've been dying to touch you. I told my sister when I got on that plane there was no way I could come here with you and not want you." She says it in a breathless rush, her admission perhaps fueled by liquor, and that's fine with me because I'm buzzed, too. Not so buzzed, though, that the sliver of text messages I've spotted locks into place.

It hits me—she's been texting her sister about me. Telling Charlotte that being near me is torture. Then

Charlotte replying that she knew Natalie would want to do this with me in Vegas. And fuck if that doesn't turn me on more.

All my reasons to resist her have vanished. All my rules separating work and pleasure have crumbled to dust. This is temporary, a one-night-only kind of tryst as we make the most of this evening.

I hope things won't be awkward in the morning, but hell, I can only think about *now*. Tomorrow is for to-morrow.

We thread through the bright lights and flashing screens in the arcade and find our way to the line for the roller-coaster. There are only a few people ahead of us. We won't have long, but I want the wait to be foreplay for her. I yank her against me, her back to my front, tugging her ass right against the outline of my hard cock.

She leans her head against my shoulder, turns her mouth to my neck, and says my name in a purr.

I whisper hers in her ear, and the way I say those three syllables seems to set her off. She pushes back into me, her sexy little ass rubbing up and down along my length. We are the fucking definition of PDA right now. We are the get-a-room people, but amazingly, no one says a thing.

Vegas, baby. I love this town.

My fingers play at the top of her skirt. "Tell me how much you want this. I want to hear you say it."

"How much I want to ride the rollercoaster?"

My hands dig into her hips. "No. How much you want me to fuck you tonight."

She spins around, her blue eyes meeting mine. She says nothing at first, just studies me. Her eyes darken with de-sire, and she never lets go of the stare. The air whooshes out of my lungs from the intensity of her gaze. "Wyatt Hammer, don't you know?"

"Don't I know what?" I say, my voice a dry husk.

Each word comes out of her mouth dripping with desire. "I ache for you."

Never have four words sounded so hot when strung together. Even though we're not alone, we might as well be. I drop my lips to hers, and for the first time all night, I kiss her softly. It lasts for a second or two, then I whisper, "You're killing me here, Nat."

Then it's our turn, and we untangle from each other as our group heads to the station with the string of yellow cars designed to look like taxi cabs.

I take no chances. I grab her hand and guide her purposefully to the last car. She slides in first, her skirt riding an inch or two up her thighs, revealing more of her smooth skin.

I join her, and as soon as we're in place, my hand is on a mission. As the cars in front of us fill up, my fingers travel to the edge of her skirt and under, then up her thighs, between her legs to the damp panel of her panties.

Then inside.

"Oh God," she gasps.

And I have two minutes and forty-five seconds to get her to say that again. And louder.

CHAPTER NINE

She spreads her legs for me, as far as she can, which isn't much, given the tight quarters of the car and the lap bar that has us locked securely in place.

But as far as I need.

She is slick and soft and so damn silky. My mouth waters because I bet she tastes amazing. The car groans its way out of the station, and I glide my fingers across all that fantastic fucking wetness. We're facing forward, and there's not much room to move, but all I need are hands and words. Even with the shoulder harness I can turn my face to her, my mouth near her ear as we begin the climb. "You weren't lying, sweetheart," I say as I slide my finger over the delicious rise of her clit.

"Lying," she says on a broken pant, "about what?"

"About the sweet torture of being near each other. This is sweet torture, indeed."

She shakes her head, and a harsh breath falls from her lips. "Not lying. Just really turned on."

"I can tell. My fingers are fucking coated in the evidence," I say as I move faster over her clit. It practically throbs under the pad of my finger.

Brisk night air greets us as the angle shifts, and we begin the ascent. Gears grind, and metal screeches against metal as the long car climbs slowly. It feels like we're at a forty-five-degree angle. Hell, maybe we are. Somehow, it works for us. Natalie squirms and pushes against my fingers as we rise.

I move faster while we chug slowly higher. I'm stroking her pussy, sliding firmly up and down her clit, following her cues. My gaze drifts to the padded lap bar. She grips it fiercely, like her life depends on it, or maybe just her pleasure. Even in this confined space, her hips rise to meet my fingers with urgency. I drag them up and down her, and she grows hotter, slicker with each stroke.

Somewhere in front of us, voices rip through the air. The wild words of anticipation. The expectation of the first big drop.

But here, my only words are for her alone as I rasp in her ear, "I want to make you come so fucking hard."

"Oh God, please. Yes. I want that," she moans as she pushes into my fingers.

We close in on the crest, and I thrust two fingers inside her. She's tight and hot, and she clenches against me. Her head drops—to hide her moans, I guess, but it's hardly necessary. We are two hundred feet in the air, and her groans are part of a chorus of sounds—whoops, hollers, and the loudest sound of all, the crank of the wheels against the tracks.

We hover at the top, all of Vegas spread out before us. Then the earth falls from us, and we plummet.

She screams. A loud, wild, thrilling yell. "Oh my God, yes," she cries out. "Like that!"

"Holy fuck!" My voice joins hers as the car hurls through the night at the speed of light, and Natalie fucks my fingers. She's a livewire, and I know she's almost there, and that nothing in the entire world is going to stop me from getting her off right now.

Desire and determination clutch me in equal measures as I work my fingers inside her while stroking her needy clit with another. Wild thing that she is, she manages to rock her hips into me, grinding and thrusting in the small space. She's just as fucking determined as I am. The urgent need to come is written in her face, in her eyelids squeezed shut. Rabid concentration is etched in her features.

I center my strokes on her clit as she begs me with whimpers and groans to keep going. Like I'd even consider stopping now.

The hollers of the other riders fill the air as we race along a corkscrew section of the tracks then blast into the loop. I'm such a horny bastard, but a lucky one, too, and I'm going to send her soaring in seconds, judging from the way her mouth is a perfect *O* as she grinds her pelvis into my hand. Then she's shrieking, and it's not just an encouraging *you're almost there, keep doing it.* It's a full-blown climax as we tip upside-down. "Oh my fucking God, oh my fucking God, oh my fucking God!" Her pussy grips me tight as she comes on my fingers.

She screams wildly as we fly through the rest of the ride. Soon her cries morph from orgasmic to joyful at the thrill of the rollercoaster. As the ride slows, she dips her head and blazes a trail of kisses up my neck as we rattle into the station, finishing them off with a nip of my earlobe, and a whisper just for me: "I can't believe we did that. That was crazy. But crazy good."

"So fucking good," I say.

Yeah, being bad is so much better.

When the car stops and the bars rise, I offer her a hand and help her out. The couple in front of us turns around, and it's the man and woman in matching Hawaiian shirts. The woman gives Natalie a wink, then me a thumbs-up.

Natalie buries her face in my shoulder, but I go with it, giving them a quick wave. "They don't call it a joy ride for nothing," I call out.

"That's for damn sure," the man says, with a proud note in his voice, like he's christened the back car of an amusement-park ride at some point or other.

Once we're inside, Natalie pulls me close and wraps her arms around my neck. She doesn't say anything. She just smiles goofily at me. "Hi."

"Hey there."

"That was . . ." Her voice trails off. Maybe she can't find the words, but the rosy glow in her cheeks and the satisfied glint in her blue eyes is enough for me.

"Interesting?" I suggest.

"It was so very interesting."

"I bet it gets even more interesting."

We resume our path, then she stops in her tracks, and points. "Look!"

I follow her finger, and a smile spreads as I spot our picture on the screen behind the counter. "So that's what we would call your *O* face."

She swats my shoulder. I grab my wallet from my back pocket, fish out a twenty, and point past the woman at the counter to the screen. "Number sixteen, please," I say, then wink at Natalie. Her forehead is in her palm. "Sixteen is the sweetest number."

The cheerful brunette with pigtails and red glasses smiles from the photo counter. "It sure is. And your sweet sixteen will be ready in a jiff. The print takes only forty-five seconds and comes with a lovely cardboard frame. Would you like it laminated too?"

I pretend to consider this. "Hmm. What do you think, Nat? Should we laminate the moment—"

She raises her face. Her eyes are fiery. "No, thank you," she says to the cheery girl. "A cardboard frame is just fine."

The girl hands me a bag and two five-by-seven close-ups of Natalie and me screaming as we flew down the tracks. As we wander out, I study them. "I suppose technically we can't be certain this is the exact moment when you came," I muse as I show her the picture.

She shoots me a stare. "It's close enough."

"Close is only good in horseshoes. Not orgasms. I mean, do we know for certain this is the moment of triumph? Should we do it again to be safe?"

She rolls her eyes. "Did you really need to buy that to mock me?"

I stop her, grabbing her arm. "I never mock orgasms. I take your pleasure seriously."

"I know," she whispers.

"Do you want me to throw them out? I will."

She softens. "I'm just giving you a hard time."

"Uh, yeah. I'd say so." My eyes swing downward, in the direction of my crotch. "You've been giving me a hard time for a long while, sweetheart."

"You are the king of puns."

"And you are the queen of the rollercoaster *O* face. But seriously, I won't show this to anyone if you don't want me to."

"Even if I wasn't about to blast off into the stratosphere of toe-curling bliss, would you honestly show that photo around? We both look like screaming idiots." She grabs it and holds it up for me, then imitates our expressions—eyes wide, mouths open, shrieking as the coaster flew along the tracks.

I shrug. "Call me crazy, but I like it. I'm going to keep them."

Then I grab the waistband of her skirt, and tug her back to me as we pass a shoot-'em-up arcade game. "Speaking of toe-curling bliss, I need to tell you that you look hot when you're coming and you look hot when you're not coming. So you're pretty much hot all the time, okay?"

She beams, and the look on her face—utter delight—does funny things to my chest. So does her voice when she answers with a simple, "Thank you." Then she adds. "I guess this would be a good time to let you know I brought along a gift for you. Only I purchased it before we even left Manhattan."

Color me intrigued.

She dips her hand into her purse, fishes around, and grabs something that she presses into my hand. The foil wrapper and the rubber ring send a bolt of heat through me.

"You're presumptuous."

She shrugs a shoulder. "But am I wrong?"

CHAPTER TEN

I'm a man with a one-track mind right now.

Since we aren't staying at this hotel, and since I need this woman like I need my next breath . . . I hunt.

With her hand in mine, I walk purposefully through the arcade, scanning, searching. Maybe there's a bathroom nearby. Or a quiet nook. Possibly a photo booth. I've always thought those are underrated hidden gems perfect for a little public action. And you'd get a souvenir photo strip too.

Then I spot a black velvet curtain near the exit of the arcade that gives me an idea. You never know what lurks behind a curtain.

Possibly, enough privacy.

I lift it, and—luck be a curtain tonight—there's some kind of storage area behind it. It's filled with out-of-commission arcade games and pinball machines.

I let the heavy material fall behind us. "You're not wrong," I say, and I kiss her again. The vodka tonic is fainter now on her lips, but the aftertaste is there, reminding me that her boldness is fueled by Bacardi and Belvedere.

But that's okay. If it weren't for the liquid courage, I wouldn't be here, either, lifting my sexy-as-fuck assistant onto a broken Metallica pinball machine.

Her hands are up my shirt in seconds. "I've wanted this for so long."

"Yeah?" I ask, inviting more, because her words are the biggest fucking turn-on of my life.

Her fingers play with the grooves in my abs. I shudder as she touches me.

"Sometimes when you come into the office, I check you out," she says in a low, sexy voice.

"Like my hair?" I joke. "You check out my hair, you mean?"

She moves in close and bites my jaw. "Your dick, Wyatt."

My skin sizzles as I spread her legs. "You pervert."

"I look at your arms and your waist, then I can't help myself. I check out your dick. Do you know you get hard at work?"

I laugh loudly. "Gee, I wonder why? Could it be the scenery? Maybe the stone-cold fox at the front desk?"

She chuckles, too. "I knew you were looking at me like you wanted to fuck me. I looked at you the same way, and all I could think was how . . . *well hung* you are." She wiggles her eyebrows then laughs louder. "That sounds so seventies porn, doesn't it?"

"Didn't you know I used to star in seventies style porn?"

She drags her index finger over my top lip. "Did you have a 'stache?"

I nod. "A proper porn 'stache. I wore super-tight jeans that flared at the bottoms. Especially when I played the pool guy or the pizza delivery man."

She hums her approval. "Maybe you can bring your VHS collection over some night, and we'll catch up on your greatest hits. Did they call you Well Hung?"

"Not only did they call me Well Hung, I had a whole series under that name." I drop my voice to an admon-ishing whisper. "But honestly, Natalie, don't you know? They were all Beta tapes. Make sure you have a Betamax machine for our movie and popcorn bow-chicka-wow-wow night."

I tug her to the edge of the pinball machine and bring her hands to the waistband of my jeans. Now I'm serious. No more joking. "That's what you were doing all those times? Wondering how it would feel to wrap your hands around my cock?"

She nods, her eyes shining with desire. "Sometimes I'd go home and just think about what it would be like to un-button your jeans, slide my hands into your boxers, and feel you in my hand."

Jesus Christ. Wildfire sparks in my veins, spreads through my blood and just fucking ignites me with more desire than I've ever felt in my life.

"Then find out," I say, dragging her hands along the button, popping it open, and guiding her fingers down the zipper. "Do it. Touch my dick."

Her eyes are hungry, as if she's about to have her biggest fantasy come true. Same for me. I'm about to fuck my Na-talie.

I push my briefs down, and when my cock springs free, Natalie's eyes widen. Her mouth falls open. "I was right," she whispers, and then opens her legs wider as she wraps a soft hand around my cock.

I hiss from the delicious fire of her touch. She rubs me up and down, her hand sliding along the long, hard, thick length of me. I nudge her legs wider as she plays. The look in her eyes is good enough to photograph. I want to remember it for a long time. Her irises are hazy with lust, and she gazes at my cock as she strokes.

She touches me like she's measuring it, weighing my dick in her hand, and I know she's satisfied. Maybe that sounds cocky, but I don't mean it that way. If she's pleased, it's because we've just admitted that we want each other with the same wild abandon, that we've both been longing for the other in the same dirty way. And that's what's so goddamn rewarding about finally touching the person you crave—it's in knowing you're both in the game, equal stakes.

She squeezes my dick hard, then rubs higher, running her fingertip over the head. I stretch my neck back, and a rumble works its way up my chest. "Fuck, Natalie. I need to be inside you. And I need it right the fuck now."

She opens the wrapper and hands the condom to me, and ten seconds later, I'm gloved up and ready for business. I scoot her an inch or two closer, position my cock at her entrance, and then push in. My brain shuts down the second my dick comes in contact with her hot, wet center. I'm only *feeling*.

It's a catalogue of spine-crackling sensations. The hot tightness. The slick wetness of her arousal that makes it so goddamn easy to slide into her. The snug fit of my dick in her pussy. How it feels like my entire body is plugged in, like I'm amped up and supercharged, because this is how a first time with someone should be.

Absolutely mind-blowing.

When we lock eyes, the pleasure moves up another level to out-of-this-world. It's so fucking intense, the way we look at each other, the connection that crackles between us.

"You are . . ." I don't even know what I'm trying to say.

"So are you . . ."

My skin sizzles from head to toe. The hair on my arms stands on end. Fuck, my nipples are hard, too. I'm aroused everywhere. She wraps her legs around my ass, hooking her ankles together, pulling me deeper. I fill her completely, my shaft coated in her all the way to the base, and I don't think my dick has ever been in a happier place. Her arms loop around my neck, and I hold her hips tight. Like that, I fuck her.

It's not a slow, lingering session of lovemaking. It's a hard and hurried screw. We could get caught. We could be arrested. We could be seen. Urgency fills the air.

One second, I'm deep in her. The next, I pull back. Then I thrust into her again, and her moans and her groans tell me she likes this rhythm. She likes the race. She likes the thrill. And as she lifts her hips to draw me back into her, she just likes the way we fit.

God, so do I. I wish I could break this down into the details, say it's the way I punch my hips, or how she grinds her sweet little pussy against my cock. But nope. It's out-of-this-world good because I want her so badly, and now I have her. And it's better than I dreamed it would be.

"Feels so good," I say.

"Feels amazing."

"You're so fucking wet."

"You're so fucking hard."

I laugh lightly as I thrust. "Guess we got the basics down."

She laughs, too, and, impossibly, that turns me on more, how *easy* the talking still is. How messing around hasn't changed a thing between us. We're still the same people.

"Think you can come again?" I don't want to be presumptuous. Maybe she's a one-and-done.

"God, I hope so," she says in a broken pant. "Think you can get me there?"

I love a good challenge. "I know so," I answer, then slide my thumb between us, rubbing her sweet clit as I stroke in and out.

"Oh God," she gasps. She drops her hands to my waist and slides her fingers up my back, under my T-shirt. "Yes, yes, yes," she says in my ear, urging me on.

I fuck, and I rub, and I focus on her. She is the center of my world.

A bead of sweat falls down my forehead. She raises her face, brushes her lips over my eyebrow, and kisses it off. That gesture sends an electric charge through me. She moans, and I'm so worked up that I know I'll be coming soon, and it will be epic. A jolt of pleasure rockets down my spine, then ripples across all my bones.

"Need to get you there," I moan, rubbing her clit, feeling her slickness on my thumb and all the fuck over my cock.

"So close, Wyatt. I'm so close. Keep doing that. Please," she begs, her voice hoarse, as if she's been screaming at a rock concert or on a rollercoaster.

And I realize that's what we are tonight. We fuck like a rock song. We screw like a wild ride that twists and turns. We are edge-of-the-seat lovers.

I jab into her with fast and powerful thrusts.

"Like that," she moans, as my thumb rubs furious circles on her clit and my cock gets to know the inside of her even better, reaching her G-spot.

She drags her nails down my back. Holy shit. She's digging in. She's scratching me. I can barely control how much I want to let go.

But she goes first, and she just detonates. She explodes with a bang, writhing and wriggling and falling apart with a loud "oh God, oh God, oh God." She drops her face onto my shoulder, muffling her moans.

But I can hear her—her sexy murmurs, her relentless cries of pleasure, and her groans of my name, again and again.

Like the chorus to that rock song.

It's just an *oh god*, over and over and over, but it's more than enough for me to blast off, too. My balls tighten, my neck goes tense, and I groan. I'm louder than I want to be, but I can't control the rumble that falls from my lips. "Gonna come," I warn, and those words turn into grunts and curses as I drive deep one last time, coming hard inside her on a pinball machine somewhere in the storage room at an arcade in a Vegas hotel.

I pant and breathe out hard. She loops her arms around my neck. The after-effects of epic pleasure hum in my bones. Damn, this is a fucking awesome night. And it's only just begun.

"You're a loud one," she says, smiling at me.

I shrug. "Loud is good."

She nods. "It is." She sighs contentedly and plays with the ends of my hair. "We're good together," she says softly, and her words take root deep inside me. They feel right. They feel true.

"Yeah, we are," I whisper. "And there's more where that came from tonight."

"Well, I certainly hope so," she says, then her lips curve up. "What's next on the agenda of Wyatt and Natalie's Excellent Adventure in Vegas?"

I stroke my chin, thinking. Then it comes to me. "I've got just the thing to show you."

CHAPTER ELEVEN

We top off on the way out of the hotel. A double round of shots for both of us keeps the night shimmering in a fine coat of a it-just-gets-better-and-better buzz.

Though, it's not just the smooth taste of Casa Noble going down that makes me feel so damn good. It's Natalie's hand in my back pocket as we leave New York-New York. It's the way she squeezes my ass as we walk along the Strip. It's how she runs her other hand through my hair while we chat.

She can't stop touching me, and it's fantastic. "You're quite the frisky mittens," I tell her as we stop at a crowded crosswalk, waiting in the throngs of tourists taking in the city of sin.

Running her fingers across the front of my T-shirt, she says, "And I get the impression you like me so . . . hands on."

"Guilty as charged." I cover her fingers with mine and drag them down my abs as far as the top of my jeans.

By the time we reach the fountains at the Bellagio, I've surpassed all ordinary levels of turned-on to the point that

I'm mildly grateful we have something to do besides touch. If she keeps up at this rate, I'm not sure how I won't be arrested for public fornication in a few minutes.

Public decency is so overrated.

I gesture grandly to the lake. "I believe this was on your Vegas Sites to See list."

She parks her palms on the railing, bouncing on her toes as she waits for the aqua extravaganza to begin. "I've wanted to see the water show here ever since I read a book that has a scene where the hero gets the heroine off in front of the railing."

Well, that's not helping my situation south of the border. "Is that your way of telling me something, Frisky Mittens?"

She laughs louder than usual and holds up two fingers. "I've got two in the bag already. I'll take my third a little later." She seems lost in thought for a moment. "Come to think of it, this writer has a bunch of books with scenes set here."

"Maybe she has a thing for the Bellagio fountains," I say as the lights splash across the placid surface and the lake begins its nighttime ballet.

Natalie gazes at the show as sprays of water dance up in the air. She sighs happily and stares at the scene before her with the contentment that only liquor can add to a night. "I can see why she likes it." She turns to me, and her tone is flirty and curious. "What do you really like?"

"Like enough to write about in a few books?"

"Sure."

"Burgers. Beer. Spicy food. But you knew all that," I say, as I pinch her ass, just because I can. She wiggles an eyebrow, and I continue, "I like sports and watching the Yankees. I like walking dogs for the rescue, helping them find homes. I enjoy random facts about the world. And I like to cook as often as I can."

A huge grin splashes across her face, and she shoves her hand on my chest. "You cook?"

I jerk my head back. "Why do you sound so shocked? I'm a man of many talents. I'll have you know I can work wonders with a grill and a skillet."

"Just surprised. I'm so used to you with your hammer and drill and that sexy-as-sin tool belt you wear," she says, roaming her eyes up and down my body, drinking me in in a way that intoxicates me more. "Now I'm picturing you cooking some delicious, spicy stir-fry in your kitchen, and since it's my fantasy, I've decided you're shirtless with a spatula."

"In my fantasy, you're wearing red panties, heels, and nothing else when I serve you this spicy stir-fry."

She shifts closer, her voice all sexy-husky as she says, "I bet it's yummy."

"Just like you," I say, wrapping my hand around her hipbone and yanking her close to me. We turn back to the water and gaze at the fountain choreography. "What about you, Frisky Mittens? What do you like so much you'd write about it in a bunch of books?"

"Besides Ed Sheeran songs?"

I shudder. "I'm going to pretend you didn't say that." She knows I can't stand the guy, but I can appreciate what he's done for scores of men by providing musical lubricant in the form of his songs.

She hums a few notes from his most popular tune then answers me. "I like being daring. I like exploring new places *and* exploring places I already know. I like being a goofball sometimes and being serious at others. I also love getting pedicures and having my toenails painted in alternating colors. And I like finally being able to live in Manhattan, because it makes me feel like anything is possible if I just keep trying."

"That's a perfect way to describe New York."

"And Vegas," she adds, meeting my eyes once more. "Turns out I like Las Vegas." She places her palm on my chest, softer this time, less Frisky Mittens, and more Sweet Natalie. "*A lot*," she adds. "I like it a lot."

An electric current swoops through me, sending warmth and desire all over my body. "Me, too." I dip my mouth to hers, brushing her lips with mine. Her soft breath ghosts over me as I pull back from the gentle kiss. "I'm really having a great time with you."

For the briefest of moments, I can see us having more conversations like this. I'm picturing spicy food competitions, exploring new corners of Manhattan, checking out all the roller coasters in the tri-state area and ticking off how many rides we can get busy on. Not because we'd be trying to amass notches in bedposts, but because it'd be fun. Natalie and I have that in common—the relentless pursuit of fun. We both like making the most of every second.

But that's not in the cards on account of that little detail of me employing her.

A flickering awareness of what might happen on Monday morning when we're back at work flashes in my brain, but then it disappears just as quickly as it arrived— because this night exists in its own bubble, and I'm having too much fun to think about anything more than the here and now.

In front of us, the aquatic show has glided into its finale, the sprays soaring high in the sky.

"Hey, let's take a selfie right now," she says, then whips out her phone, swinging it wildly into shooting position. I crowd in close and wrap an arm around her. We smile for the camera, framed in the background by one of the prettiest sights in all of Vegas.

"Now, let's get you to the Venetian, and grab the next gondola." I smack her ass.

She wiggles her eyebrow. "I like that."

"You are so fucking interesting, Little Bo Peep."

"Just wait till you see my crook."

As we head to the Venetian, she posts the image of us together on her Facebook page. A crew of women out on the town walks in our direction. One of them sips on a towering drink that looks like an oversize beaker from a chemistry class. Natalie stares at it longingly after she puts her phone away.

"Ever had one of those in Vegas?" I say to her.

She elbows my ribs. "You know I haven't."

"Then we need to deflower you in the 'towering, delicious-looking cocktail that you down on the street' department." As the group nears us, I call out, "Hey there. Just wondering where we can grab one of those fantastic concoctions."

The woman points to a street cart on the next block, where we order one. And it turns out this beaker is full of the good shit.

Natalie taps the pink plastic container shaped like a bong. "This is like a fast track to a super-buzz."

"Yeah, it pretty much goes straight to the brain. Probably the judgment center," I joke, then hum a line from the

Sheeran number she sang earlier. "Definitely the judgment center."

As we walk along the canal shops, my arm draped over her shoulders, we tell dirty jokes, sing snippets of favorite songs, and laugh so hard I'm not sure we can stop.

"Hey, want to hear something funny?"

"Duh. Of course I do."

"When I was in middle school, there was a rumor going around that if you laughed for twenty-four hours straight, you'd get a six-pack. Like, it was a one-time thing. If you could pull this off for a full day, you'd be set for life, all carved and shit," I say, gesturing to my belly.

She cracks up then slides her fingers over the fabric of my shirt. "Did you do a laugh-a-thon to get these?"

"No, but we tried it at home," I admit, sheepishly.

She clutches her belly, cracking up. "Oh my God, you're ridiculous."

"We decided to watch the funniest shows on TV, and Nick and I found these cartoons he was totally into. Some Japanese animated thing that was fucking hilarious. We managed about fifteen minutes of non-stop laughing." Then I pull her close. "But I've laughed a lot tonight, so maybe I'm finally getting a twelve-pack."

She shakes her head. "Not gonna happen."

I pout. "Why not?"

"Because soon, you're going to stop laughing."

"Are you going to tell me something sad?"

Another shake. "Nope. But I'm pretty sure you won't be laughing when we're naked later. You'll be moaning and groaning and making those sexy sounds you make when you lose control for me."

And the temperature in me shoots through the roof. I do groan as I tug her close.

"Just. Like. That," she says in a sexy purr.

I cup the back of her head and kiss her like crazy. We both sound like we can't get enough of each other.

When we manage to untangle, I guide her to the gondola ride. We settle on the seat as a man in a striped shirt and a red beret pushes a giant pole-like oar through the water. I wrap my arm around Natalie, and out of nowhere, I start humming that same tune again. And it hits me—I would never sing this sober. I would never sing it buzzed.

Which means, I'm not buzzed.

I'm borderline drunk.

And the world is my oyster.

Evidently, it's everyone's oyster tonight, because there's clapping and cheering from the other gondolas. I swing my eyes around to the boat in front of us. A dude in pressed pants and a white button-down shirt has dropped to one knee, and a brunette has her arms around his neck and is crying happy tears as she gazes at a new ring on her finger. I watch as the afterglow of a proposal unfolds around us. Everyone else is cheering for them, too. Onlookers from the banks of the canals offer their hoots and hollers, and so does Natalie.

She cups her hands around her mouth. "Woohoo!"

She nudges me, and that's my cue to chime in, too, so I pump a fist and shout, "Congrats! Go marry her tonight!"

The guy laughs, and shoots me a thumbs-up. His bride-to-be waves at us. Someone walking along the shops seconds my idea. "Go to A Little White Wedding Chapel!"

In their gondola, the button-down guy and his lady lock eyes, and seem to be weighing the idea, whispering to each other. A few seconds later, he holds his arms out wide. "We're getting married tonight!"

The cheers erupt, this time like your favorite slugger just knocked in a bottom-of-the-ninth game-winning home-run. Natalie's shouts are the loudest, and she grabs my arm as she calls out boisterously, "They're going to the chapel, and they're gonna get married . . ." She slinks her arm tight around my waist. "Because you convinced them to tie the knot tonight."

"When in Vegas . . ." I say, and my voice trails off as our eyes meet.

Those three words echo.

Her eyes sparkle, and it's like we're thinking the same damn thing.

I like being daring.

"Exactly how daring do you like to be?" I ask.

One corner of her lips curves up. "Exactly as daring as I can be. Why do you ask?"

"Because of our deal for tonight. To do it all. One night only." I tip my forehead to the couple, and I swear I've never had a better idea in the history of ideas than the one I have right now. It's fucking genius. "Are you thinking what I'm thinking?"

Her mouth drops open, then she nods, her eyes wild with excitement. "I'm pretty sure I might be. Want to tell me what you're thinking?"

I raise an eyebrow. "I'm thinking there's one more thing that would make this the full Vegas experience."

She clasps one hand to her mouth then lets go. "Oh my God. Are we really going to do what they're doing?"

"I don't see that we have a choice, given the deal we made back at the New York-New York bar. Go big or go home."

For a moment, there's nothing but silence. I don't have to wait long for an answer, though.

"Go big, Wyatt," she says, her voice soft, but her intention loud. Clearly, she thinks my idea is brilliant, too. How could she not?

Dropping down to one knee, I grab her hand. "Frisky Mittens, want to go to a twenty-four-hour chapel and tie the knot?"

She hiccups, then laughs and tugs me in for a sloppy kiss that tastes like tequila and fruit mixer. "When in Vegas . . ."

CHAPTER TWELVE

One sideburn slides off the man's face.

It's mildly distracting. But nowhere near as disturbing as the officiant's gold leisure suit. The one-piece has a collar that could double as wings, and is the very definition of skintight. It hugs every inch of his body, and yeah, I do mean *inch*.

Sorry, not sorry. He's wearing a fucking unitard. Hard not to notice shit.

"Is he Leisure Suit Larry or Elvis?" I hiss to Natalie. When the venue has a name like Larry, Lana, and the King's Full-Service Quickie Weddings, he could be either.

She nods at the guy, who's got a full perm going on, taking kinky curls to new heights, and whispers to me, "Or Richard Simmons got a new gig."

Only it's not a true whisper. It's a drunk whisper. So she's not quiet in the least, but I doubt the exercise fanatic double cares, since I'm pretty sure he's stoned. Looks that way, as he fumbles around for the wedding bands while we stand at the front of the tiny chapel. That's part of the full service—two gold bands for fifty-seven bucks. What a steal.

He reeks of pot, and judging from the Bob Marley tune playing as our wedding music this second, I'm guessing he was toking up before the limo dropped us off a few minutes ago, right after we grabbed a marriage license before those offices closed at midnight. The swanky black stretch number waits for us in the lot. I sprung for the best on my wedding night. That's just the kind of swell fellow I am.

Fishing around in the breast pocket of his suit, the dude grabs the rings, and holds them up. "'Got 'em." One slips from his fingers. "Oopsy daisy."

That sends Natalie into peals of laughter, and she grabs my arms, clutching me as she holds on. I chuckle, too, because everything is funny tonight. And everything is awesome, like my life is bobbing on a raft in an infinity pool under the warm sun, drinking a piña colada without a care in the world.

Natalie runs her hands up and down my arms, and I wiggle my eyebrows. We can't stop flirting, touching, giggling.

The dude bends to fetch the ring when I hear the telltale sign of stitches coming undone. I'm not sure what part of the leisure suit has popped open, but I decide to keep my eyes fixed firmly on the bride-to-be, just in case Larry Elvis Officiant is a commando-style guy.

"That's the real oopsy daisy," Natalie says, and now I'm the one to crack up, grasping her trim little waist in my hands. Nothing quite like laughing like a hyena at your own nuptials.

"All set now," the guy says, and then he cups his hand to the side of his mouth and shouts, "Hey Lana! Can we get some grand finale music?"

A woman in a white Elvis suit, her breasts spilling out from the mostly unzipped zipper, pops in and gives a big thumbs-up. "Oh, look at the happy couple," she coos, then points overhead. Maybe to the sound system at the chapel, which now pipes in the opening bars of a song I recognize as soon as I hear the first line about what wise men say.

A strange thing happens to my chest again when I turn back to Natalie in my arms. It's like my heart is being squeezed. I blink, trying to center myself, but it's hard when she's staring at me as Leisure Suit Larry clears his throat, and the King croons in this most romantic song about fools rushing in. I kind of feel like I'm floating. Must be all the liquor playing tricks on me, making me smile like an idiot as Natalie looks at me, her eyes big and full.

The officiant hands me her band, and Natalie and I move apart briefly as he runs through the familiar vows. We exchange rings, and as I stare at my newly adorned finger, something unnamed bubbles up inside me. I step closer to Natalie once more, clasp her hands in mine, and words tumble out in a rush. I'm telling her how gorgeous she is, and how much I've loved working with her, and how ridiculously fun this night is, and then I'm saying all sorts of things about what the future holds, and doesn't hold, and I can barely keep track of everything I'm saying. I'm just serving up all that feels true, past, present, and future. She nods vigorously the whole time, and I love this about her—she fucking *gets* me. Then, that unnamed thing in me shifts, and now it tightens, ratcheting into worry. Before I know it, I tell her the most important thing I've ever told her. And I find myself making her promise to hold me to it.

"Just promise me, Nat. Promise me, promise me, promise me," I say with a harsh swallow, and then I wait.

But not for long.

"I promise, Wyatt. I promise. I promise. And I get it. I do. I really do."

The momentary tension inside me vanishes in an instant, and my world is all hazy, sexy, intoxicating goodness once more.

I put my hands on her face and then kiss my wife for the first time—a searing, deep, passionate kiss that's a reminder of how utterly fucking amazing this night has been. She sways slightly as I kiss her, and I wobble then find my footing, and we separate at last, grinning like fools rushing in.

The officiant clears his throat. "There is no more dwelling at the Heartbreak Hotel for Natalie and Wyatt, and now these two are stuck on each other. By the powers vested in me by the great state of Nevada, and by the King himself, I now pronounce Natalie and Wyatt husband and wife. But remember there is no return to sender. So, it's time for you all to get shook up. You're married!" He thrusts his gold-satin covered arms in the air and hoots. "I would tell you to kiss the bride, son, but you already did, and I bet you've done a helluva lot more. So be on your way, and do some more of that!"

A few minutes later, we slide into the limo. I pop open the champagne and toast to my bride as we drive around town after midnight, getting horizontal again. Soon, we stop at the Flamingo for roulette. When we win a round, a tipsy dude at our table who says he works for a rapper invites us to a party in the penthouse suite.

"You guys are cool. You gotta come check out Secretariat's bash," he says, running his big palm over his shaved head.

We cash out and go, because why the fuck not?

Especially, since the rapper named himself for a Triple Crown winner.

On the top floor of the hotel, the party rages. Music pulses so loudly it thrums in my bones, as scantily-clad women grind against scantily-clad men, and another group of partygoers ride hobby horses as they chug their drinks. Natalie and I take it all in, then check out the view of the Strip, and enjoy the free-flowing champagne.

Natalie cups her hand around my ear. "Need to find the little girl's room."

That sounds like a fine idea to me too, and when we've both answered nature's call, she peers down the hallway at the end of the suite and points.

Holy shit.

"There's a fucking Titanic slot machine in the penthouse," I say, heading straight for it, parked next to a standard Las Vegas slot machine with fruit on the screen.

"Wanna play? It takes bills," she says.

We slide some dollars into its mouth, and proceed to lose all our roulette winnings. But it hardly feels like losing when Natalie parks herself on my lap and wraps her arms around me as Jack, Rose, and a Heart of the Ocean spin into view.

Feels a lot like winning when her lips crush mine, and her hands slide down my chest. All sense of propriety slinks around the corner, as I check to make sure the coast is clear, pull her behind the slot machine, and make good use of another one of those condoms she so thoughtfully packed for our trip. She must have brought a box.

As I hike up her leg around my hip and drive deeper, I whisper in her ear. "You're so fucking daring."

"And you're so fucking interesting," she says on a moan.

As she grows louder, nearing the edge, I cover her mouth since someone's now in the hallway with us, yanking the other one-armed bandit. Whoever it is nails three cherries, right as Natalie lands her third climax of the evening.

Guess we're all getting lucky tonight.

We say goodbye to Secretariat and the bald-headed dude, thanking them profusely for their hospitality, as well as the wonderfully convenient height of the slot machines. Good thing they were so damn tall and provided just enough cover. Once we leave, we cruise down the Strip and take a selfie at the famous Vegas sign. Natalie posts that on Facebook, too. And we dance dirty at the Edge nightclub at a newer hotel. Sometime after four thirty, we make it back to her room. Or maybe it's mine. I honestly don't know. The night is a blur. A streak of laughter and sex and wild, crazy fun.

All I know for certain when we stumble into the suite with the king-sized bed is that this night is far from over. Not when she looks at me with sultry eyes while her busy fingers make quick work of her shirt and skirt.

My hands cover hers, stopping her. "I'll take it from here. It's time for me to fuck my wife."

It will be the first time I see her naked, and I'm like a kid on Christmas morning. There's nothing I want more than the gift of Mrs. Hammer's nudity.

CHAPTER THIRTEEN

Generally speaking, all sex is good sex.

It's a guy thing. Honestly, it's just anatomically difficult for us to have bad sex. Enough friction, along with a little something wet on the equipment, and chances are good we'll achieve the big bang. That's the nice thing about being a dude.

But some sex is better than others, and at the pinnacle is hotel sex. The dark of the night, the size of the bed, the escape from reality . . . hotel rooms are designed for great sex.

Nothing could be truer for Natalie and me right now, here on the last stop of our great escape.

Neon from the Las Vegas night casts a faint light, illuminating her face, silhouetting her body. She's perched on the edge of the bed.

A part of me wants to undress her slowly, to savor every slide of silk and lace along her smooth, soft skin. But a stronger part of me knows now's not the time for lazy, unhurried, we-have-all-night foreplay. The red lights on the hotel radio remind me that it's not long before the sun comes up, so I tuck all the images of slow kisses along her calves and lingering caresses across her belly out of my mind.

Besides, her tits are pretty much calling my name. The low-cut cups of her black lacy bra expose succulent, kissable, bitable pale flesh. In mere seconds, they'll be free, and I'm not sure I'll be able to take my hands off them. I think I'm in love with them already.

"Can't believe I haven't gotten acquainted with these beauties yet tonight," I say as I unhook her bra with a quick snap. "But no time like the present to rectify that."

As I throw her bra behind me, the lace falls somewhere, but I don't notice or care because her tits are now liberated, and I was right.

It's fucking love at first sight. My hands dart out to cup her breasts, and yep, it's love at first touch, too, because *damn.* They feel spectacular. Evidently, it feels good to her, too, since she gasps as I squeeze and knead. I rub my calloused fingers over her nipples and pinch. Her hands shoot out to my hair. She threads her fingers through the strands and grips me tight, saying my name like a long, low moan. "That turns me on so much," she murmurs.

Holy hell, Natalie has insanely sensitive nipples, and I adore her tits. Who would have predicted a more perfect union? Maybe my hands should marry her breasts.

"You won't mind if I just verify precisely how turned on you are?" I tease.

"Please feel free to conduct a proper and thorough test . . . Inspector Hammer," she says with a grin.

I laugh as I run a hand down her belly, then, as I slide my palm between her thighs, I stop laughing. Even I can't make a joke about this kind of wetness because it's just too fucking fantastic. She's soaked through her panties.

Beautifully soaked.

I crowd against her, my big body pushing hers down to the bed. She crawls back and props herself on her elbows. I climb over her, my clothes still on.

I lower my head to her chest, draw a nipple into my mouth, and suck hard. She bucks up against me as I lick and suck and kiss her nipples. This is the true jackpot— learning my woman likes having her nipples played with.

She moans, and groans, and grabs my head again.

She's got me in a headlock, and trust me, this girl knows how to execute that move, but there's no way I'm letting go of this beautiful breast in my mouth. Nothing to worry about there. You'd have to pry me off from this taste of heaven. She widens her legs and rocks up into me as I draw her nipple deeper, flicking my tongue against it, then biting down. She lets out a little shout.

"That drives me crazy," she moans, never letting go of me, and I wonder momentarily if she could actually come from this kind of play. Seems like a far-fetched fantasy, but I'd be willing to go the distance and find out. As I devour her breast, my hand squeezes the other tit, kneading, pinching, and pulling until Natalie thrashes under me.

Jesus Christ, this woman is more than *interesting* in bed. She's electric. She's wild. She's so damn sensual and in touch with her body. It's addictive, the way she wants what I want. She pushes my head away and stares at me. Her eyes are crazed, hungry, as she jams her hands between us, hunting for my jeans and fumbling for the zipper. "Now, Wyatt. I need you now. I need you inside me."

There are just certain words that cause instantaneous action in a man. No matter what else you're doing, when a woman says, "I need you inside me," you stop, drop, and answer the call.

In seconds, Natalie's shed her panties, and I'm naked too, rubbing the head of my dick against the slick paradise of her pussy. She grabs my ass. Her hands on me make my head spin. Fuck, I want her so much. Tonight won't be enough to quench this desire.

I start to push into her, when I realize my dick is bareback.

"Shit," I curse, hanging my head low.

"What is it?"

"Condom. Need to get one."

But her hands grip me harder. "I'm on the pill. Are you safe?"

I nod. "Clean as a whistle."

"Same here." She lifts her face and brings her lips to my ear. "I think my husband can fuck me without a condom."

And that does it. Something about the way those words fall from her mouth in such an inviting purr makes it impossible for me to resist.

I sink into her, and it's staggering. She's hot and tight, and the wetness is infinitely more wonderful because I feel it with no barriers. Skin against skin. Hardness against heat. Her and me. She raises her knees and hooks her ankles against my lower back, and I pump. I shove in and out of her. Watching her face. Studying her reaction. Loving the way she breathes out hard and groans.

She's so noisy, and her sounds are a drug. I love that she can't hold back. That she's a moaner, and an "oh god"-er, and a "yes, just like that"-er. Makes my job so much easier to know what the lady likes.

And by all accounts, the lady likes it when I fuck her. When I drive in deep. When I stroke back, nearly pulling out of her. And when I drop my face to the Candy Land of her tits again, sucking on each nipple till she moans.

When I let go, I move my mouth to her neck, nipping her. My reward is her lifting her hips faster and wilder as her noises go into overdrive.

I take her with deep, fast thrusts. "Love this. Love your hot, wet pussy," I rasp out. "Fucking love fucking you."

"Love it, too," she says in a broken pant.

Sweat slicks our chests, and the room fills with the sounds of *us*. Flesh slapping, feral grunts, guttural cries, and the bed smacking the wall. This is hotel sex. This is the furious race along the fast track to a fiery release.

She wriggles and writhes, then she drags her nails down my back.

"Leave marks," I tell her, like a command.

"I'm going to," she says, digging in deeper and scratching my flesh in a way that sends heat spiraling in every corner of my body. I like it rough. I like the evidence of rough sex, too.

She lifts her head and kisses me, a hard and hungry kiss, full of teeth and need. We claw at each other's mouths as I pound into her, and she urges me on with thrusts that meet mine, and nails that dig into my ass.

When our lips lose contact, her blue eyes lock on mine, and they're so honest, so full of desire.

And they disarm me. They strip me of all my defenses. They threaten to undo all the reasons I know we can't make this last beyond tonight. They make my heart beat harder, and I slow down.

I ease the pace.

I take a break from the relentlessness of our lovemaking. So does she, as her hands quit scratching. Instead, they travel along my back, up to my neck, and into my hair, making me shudder.

The noises between us fade to just breathing, just husky moans. My hand reaches for her hip, and I hike her leg up higher as I slow-fuck her. I lower to my elbows, and I stare into her eyes. She trembles. Her whole body shudders.

"Oh God, Wyatt," she whispers.

She's not loud and crazy. She's just raw and real now, and I feel the same way. Naked, totally fucking naked, and not just because I'm in my birthday suit.

But because it hits me hard—no matter what tomorrow brings, tonight I'm fucking my wife. I bring my mouth to her ear, and murmur, "I love fucking my wife. God, I love fucking my wife so much."

It's the truth. Nothing but the truth.

And she cries out.

She shatters, shaking under me, as a barely comprehensible series of "oh God," and "I'm coming," and "I'm coming so fucking hard" fall from her lips. I love that she can't control her mouth, that words of pleasure spill forth as she falls apart beneath me, like a category-five orgasm has swept through her body, unleashing wave after crashing wave of ecstasy. Her release flips the switch in me. My quads tighten. My balls squeeze. And pleasure surges like a storm in my body, spreading everywhere, my own groans now loud enough to wake the neighbors.

"Fuck, Natalie," I moan, as I come inside her. "Jesus. Fucking. Christ."

Every word punctuates the intensity that lights me up as my body jerks, and I can't stop moaning, or groaning, or swearing. "Fucking hell," I say on a long pant as I collapse on her.

Her arms loop around me. "You're so loud," she says. "Do you have any idea how hot it is when you come like that?"

I laugh lightly. "Glad you enjoy what you do to me."

"Nothing is sexier than knowing I made you moan."

"Except you. You're sexier," I say, and then I raise my face to brush my lips lightly against hers when something occurs to me.

Yes, all sex is good, but not all sex is created equally. I'm not just talking about hotel sex. Because I've just learned that sex with Natalie is in a class of its own. It's beyond hotel sex. It's more than the bee's knees. It's better than the cat's meow.

It's heart-stoppingly magnificent.

And I'm not the kind of guy who uses that word.

But sex with her is indeed magnificent.

I'm sweating and panting and totally spent, and I'm pretty sure you can wring alcohol from my pores, but this has been a night for the ages. I tug her close, brush her hair from her cheek, and tell her, "Nobody in the history of Vegas has done this city as well as we have."

She smiles. "And nobody ever will."

And I'm sure when I look back on this night, I'm going to savor every single delicious detail.

CHAPTER FOURTEEN

Natalie: Remember *The Hangover*? That morning-after scene?

Charlotte: Is this your way of telling me you're missing a tooth? Because I'm not okay with that. You have very nice white, straight teeth.

Natalie: Ha. The fangs are fine. My head still hurts, but my throat got intimately acquainted with some aspirin and a coffee chaser already, so I'm surviving the after-effects. Now, try again.

Charlotte: Oh, wait! Bradley Cooper is shirtless in your suite?

Natalie: Nope. But a girl can dream :)

Charlotte: Um, Zach Galifianikas is . . . pantsless?

Natalie: One more guess.

Charlotte: There's a tiger in your tub?

Natalie: I'm taking away your movie card. Moving on . . .

Charlotte: *insert epic eye roll* Did you use all, some, or none of the six-pack of raincoats you brought along? Did you get drunk with your boss? Kiss your boss? Sleep with your boss? Spend the night with your boss?

Natalie: We used nearly all. Which means yes to all of the above. And there's something I've got tell you.

Charlotte: !!!!!!!! Tell me everything now. Start with the good stuff. HOW WAS THE DEED?

Natalie: It was amazing. Look, everything was amazing. Well, one thing wasn't. But I'll get to that.

Charlotte: What??? Does he have bad breath? Ugly toes? Does he fart in his sleep?

Natalie: NO!!!!! NO!!!! NO!!!

Charlotte: Then what would be bad?

Natalie: First, the good stuff. The kissing, the talking, the laughing. We get along so well. He cracks me up. He cares about me. He's good to me. And he kisses me like . . . well, like I've always wanted to be kissed.

Charlotte: Swoon . . . Like the world will end and nothing else matters but the kiss?

108 · LAUREN BLAKELY

Natalie: Yes. And the sex. Oh dear God, the sex. Beyond anything I could imagine.

Charlotte: And you have a good imagination.

Natalie: I do, I do, I do. It was just all so good. But there's something I have to tell you.

Charlotte: You didn't come?

Natalie: No, I didn't stop coming. I lost track. I had twenty orgasms. Maybe six. But it felt like twenty. Or two hundred.

Charlotte: So what's the problem? Well, besides the little issue of him being your boss and you being his employee and I therefore being a very bad sister for encouraging you to pursue the man you're totally hot for? Since everyone knows boss-employee relationships are a massive no-no and always end up in heartbreak. But if anyone breaks your heart, I will kick him in the balls twenty times because I love you like crazy. Bottom line—am I kicking him in the balls?

Natalie: I *might* have married him last night. (Hello? Don't you remember Ed Helms waking up married?)

.

.

.

.

.

.

.

Natalie: Um. Hello? Are you there? Bueller?

Charlotte: &*$#%^

Charlotte: TELL ME YOU ARE KIDDING.

Charlotte: Tell me that's one of your patented Natalie-is-pulling-my-leg-jokes???

Natalie: Don't yell at me! It makes my head hurt!

Charlotte: I will damn well yell at you for something like this! And why didn't you tell me sooner?

Natalie: I was trying to, but then we got to the sex questions. Anyway, relax. I panicked a little when I woke up, but after the caffeine and aspirin helped me recover some of my lost brain cells, I already have a plan to fix this.

Charlotte: I can't believe you married him. I know you're hot for him. But are you fucking insane????

Natalie: We were just really drunk.

Charlotte: Well, *unmarry* him. Like, now.

Natalie: I will. Obviously.

Charlotte: How did it happen?

Natalie: The officiant said "I now pronounce you hound dog and wife." Or something like that.

Charlotte: Not the actual ceremony. I KNOW how vows go down. I meant EVERYTHING LEADING UP TO IT.

Natalie: We were on the gondola. Someone else proposed. We decided to do it, too. It seemed like a brilliant, fun, amazing idea at the time, like all ideas do when you've had a half-dozen drinks. So we got married. Then we had more sex. In the limo. Behind a slot machine. But before then it was on a pinball machine. And kinda on a rollercoaster, too.

Charlotte: Fine, you get a medal for Outstanding Achievement in Public Sex. And I get that it was the best sex of your life, but you can't let it fry your brain, hon. I mean, date him maybe, Nat. But don't marry him.

Natalie: Don't worry. We won't be married much longer. And we won't be dating, either.

Charlotte: Why??? Forget everything I said above about it being a bad idea. You said he's good to you. Why not date?

Natalie: Shoot. He's waking up. I'll tell you when I get back to New York.

Charlotte: Dying here waiting . . .

CHAPTER FIFTEEN

The big orb in the sky blares angrily through the window, shooting bright bolts of light that assault my eyes. I squeeze my lids, rubbing them, trying to will away the relentless sunshine attack.

But my head . . .

When did my head start doing an impression of a cannonball? Wait. No, it feels more like a construction zone, and an army of small angry men are jackhammering inside my skull. I groan and fling an arm over my eyes.

A small voice speaks softly. "Hey, time to get up."

I wince, not from the voice, but from reality. Reality sucks. My mouth is sawdust. My veins slog with mud. My head weighs fifty tons.

Hangovers are fun, said no one ever.

"Sleeping beauty," the voice whispers, accompanied by a gentle shake on my shoulder.

I scoot up in bed, drag a hand through my messy hair, then cover my mouth as I yawn and . . . *What the fuck is this on my left hand???*

I sit bolt upright, cannonball-brain be damned.

I lift my hand as if it's been sewn on by extraterrestrials in my sleep. Because there's a motherfucking gold band on my finger.

Yup. Aliens. UFOs. Martians. That's the only reasonable explanation. Little green men visited me last night and shoved a wedding ring on my finger.

I turn my head slightly and see a blonde in my bed. She must be the owner of the soft voice. Or maybe she's an angel. Looks like one. The sun shines brightly, and I squint, but I can see she's smiling, a little wistfully. Damn, she's pretty, and her eyes are the warmest shade of blue I've ever seen. I cover my mouth because my breath must be dumpster levels now, and infecting a lovely like her with morning mouth is a crime.

I blink.

Holy shit.

That's my assistant in my bed, dressed in a gray tank top and jeans, with her wet hair twisted in a bun on top of her head.

And I'm dressed like I'm about to go skinny-dipping.

I scratch my head. Maybe I called her last night. Begged her to come rescue me from whatever shenanigans I'd gotten myself into with whoever is wearing the other half of this pair of rings. Man, I've no clue who I married last night, or when Natalie, ever efficient and super organized, arrived to save my ass. Maybe I'm still drunk.

Note to self: Exhibit a bit more decorum with employees in the future.

"Need to brush my teeth," I say, and scramble out of bed.

Scramble may be an exaggeration. More like drag my sorry, hungover ass out of bed. Oh. Right. Naked ass, too. I really need to work on decorum, stat.

But nature calls. In the bathroom, I take an epic piss that lasts so long I might need to call Guinness and enter it in Longest Whizzes Ever. While I'm at it, I'd like to campaign to change the phrase *take a piss* to *leave a piss* because no one actually takes pee.

I flush, wash my hands, and brush the morning-after stink-breath from my mouth.

Better. I'm semi-human now.

Nah, that's too generous. More like one-quarter human. I run the faucet, splash cold water on my face and into my eyes, and stare in the mirror. Then at my ring. Then back in the mirror.

"What the fuck did you do last night, Hammer?" I mutter.

Natalie's eyes flash back at me in the reflection. I spin around and wince, groaning as the drilling in my head resumes.

She holds a cup of coffee in one hand and points to the marble counter with the other. "There's aspirin. I set some out for you when I got up and had mine. Looks like you need it."

I grab the two white pills, toss them on my tongue, and send them down the hatch, on a mercy mission to take away the pain. She thrusts the coffee at me. "Since you're a coffee whore," she says with a knowing little wink.

I take it and thank her. She is part-angel, after all. I drink some of the life-sustaining substance, and its restorative powers begin to kick in. Maybe I'm closing in on halfway human now.

"You okay?" Her voice is gentle, caring. "I didn't feel so hot when I woke up, either. But I'm managing better now."

I shrug, trying to play it cool, which is not helped by the fact that I'm swinging free this morning. She doesn't seem fazed by my lack of pants, though. Must really give this woman a raise. She's unflappable. She's gone above and beyond the call of duty. "Yeah, sure. And sorry about all this." I gesture to my crotch, which is heading into morning wood territory.

She shoots me a tiny grin.

Jesus Christ.

Could I possibly cross any more lines of inappropriate behavior with her? My eyes land on her left hand, and the matching ring.

My heart stops pumping. My breath stutters. The floor falls out.

I squeeze my eyes shut. No way. No way. *No way.* This is just a dream. A very vivid dream. I haven't actually crossed *that* line. But when I open my eyes, she's here, I'm here, and so are the rings. My heart gallops away from my chest and steals my sanity with it.

I point.

Gawk.

Try to speak.

"What the . . .?"

She parks her hand on her hips. "What? Is there a tiger in the tub?"

"Huh?"

"Are you missing a tooth?"

My hand goes to my mouth. No, please God no—I have nightmares about that. I love my teeth. Years of braces set them straight, and now they're a fantastic set of gleaming choppers. Running my fingers over them, I breathe a sigh of relief. Whew. They're all good. "Teeth are fine."

"Or is *this* the thing freaking you out?" She holds up her hand, brandishing the matching band once more. "You married me last night, dingdong." She rolls her eyes. They're a bit red, like she didn't get much more sleep than I did. "I can't believe you don't remember."

"Noooo," I say coolly, lying my fucking ass off. "I remember everything. It's all crystal clear."

She cocks her head, studying me. "Is it?"

I drag a hand along the back of my neck, determined to get a handle on the big, fat blank inside my mind. "Yeah. It's in Technicolor up here," I say, tapping my head.

"That's great, then. You won't be surprised when the cops show up shortly to take a statement about how you stripped to your birthday suit, jumped into the Bellagio Fountains and shouted, 'Join me, Frisky Mittens.'"

Ding, ding, ding.

That's it. With those words, bits and pieces of last night surface. I remember a sideburn, a rollercoaster, her frisky hands, a towering drink, a crazy proposal, and then my head spins. I sway, grabbing the sink. More comes into focus. The fucking and the kissing and the talking and then the brilliant idea, like we'd never had a better one in the world, to get married.

And so we did.

Because . . . we were drunk in Vegas.

Holy shit.

I kissed my assistant.

I banged my assistant.

I married my assistant.

I broke my one big fat rule. Because I don't, as in never fucking ever, mix business and pleasure. But by all accounts, last night I stomped on that rule in spectacular fashion.

"Oh, and apparently there's a viral video circulating of you climbing up the Vegas sign," she adds. "Like a tree monkey."

She's fucking with me, but rather than let on that I'm reeling, I adopt my best playful smile. "I'm agile, but I'm not that agile, sweetheart. I'd need suction cups on my hands to pull that off." In an effort to regain some memory cred with her, I rattle off, "Maybe if you'd told me I climbed a rollercoaster I'd believe you. Or a pinball machine."

I just can't fathom that those fiestas of fucking led to a proposal, and I can't stop staring at my finger, either, like the longer I look, the greater the chance it'll disappear. But it's not conducting a vanishing act, even though the details of the wedding itself are just a blur, like a streak of neon across the night. I can recall a guy in a tight gold leisure suit, some Elvis tunes, laughing like crazy with Natalie, then a speedy "I do." Next, a ride in a limo, toasting, sticking our heads out the window, the night air blasting our faces and cooling us off from the heat of all that . . . screwing.

A memory of the sounds she made when she came blasts through my brain, like a chorus of her pleasure, stirring my cock to full salute.

Why, oh why, did the sex with her have to be so ridiculously sublime?

She taps her wrist. "Our flight leaves in two hours, Sleeping Beauty. I did a little research before you got out of bed, and it looks like there's just enough time for you to shower and for us to get an annulment, grab a car to the airport, and make our departure. I checked us into our flight already, and we can just go to TSA pre-screen since we're first class," she says, brushing one palm against the other.

My mind spins with whiplash. We got married last night, and Natalie has already arranged the exodus from that bad decision? How does she do this? She yawns, the only other evidence that last night took a toll on her, too, but then she returns to normal in a heartbeat. Damn, she has impressive hangover recovery skills.

"You found someone already?" I shouldn't be surprised. This is what she does. She's impeccably organized and a master planner. Still, this is a new level of efficiency even for her.

"I did. We'll be unmarried before you know it," she says, then makes a shooing gesture. "Move it along."

"Did you book the annulment before we even tied the knot?" I say, trying to make a joke. "Admit it—you brought me here planning to get me down the aisle and have your wicked way with me. You tricked me, didn't you?"

But judging from the furrow of her brows, I've failed miserably in the humor department. "Tricked you?"

"Yeah. So you could have me all night long."

She sighs heavily. "That would imply I'd intended to marry you last night."

"Wait. Whose idea was it, then?"

She stares at me like the words coming out of my mouth are foreign. Maybe they are. When she speaks, her tone is laced with frustration. "Both. We got married because we were drunk and daring and having fun, not because *I* planned it," she says, tapping her chest. "We both woke up hungover. We both woke up shocked. I'm simply the one trying to untangle the mess we both made and make sure we still get home on time. Thanks to my amazing googling skills, as well as my astonishing ability to wake up before you, I accomplished that. Not through some feat of supreme trickery. Anyway, I tracked down a paralegal that's not too far out of the way as we head to the airport. The car service will be here in thirty minutes. Now, if you'll excuse me, I need to blow-dry my hair."

She turns on her heel. But before she leaves, she snaps her gaze back to me then roams her eyes down my body. "By the way, nice boner. In case you forgot that part of last night, we screwed four times, and you came harder and louder than I'm sure you ever did before."

She leaves, and my feet are glued to the tiles of the bathroom, and my dick points in her direction, wanting a repeat.

"Down, boy," I mutter, but my dick doesn't listen because what she just said was fucking hot. So were all those orgasms last night.

"You were loud, too," I call out as I trudge to the shower, turn it on high, and try to wash off the regret. Because as hot as the sex was, I was sure I'd moved on from my stint of bad choices with women. I'd been to rehab, I'd learned my lesson, and I'd followed my own guidelines.

Till last night.

When I fell off the wagon big time.

I bend my head under the stream, letting the hot water scald my neck and run down my back. As I soap up, a blast of memories fights its way to the front of my head, reminding me of the two big mistakes in my past when it comes to women. I picture Roxy, her sexy smirk that won me, then the letter from her years later trying to rip me to shreds. Given how all the shit went down with her, I was cautious and careful with Katrina. Little good it did. The bitch hacked me anyway.

My chest tightens painfully as I picture that sweet, blond beauty in the other room doing the same. Natalie could skewer me and have my business for lunch. She's Mrs. Hammer now. She's got access to what's mine, and I can't stop imagining her taking my credit card numbers, stealing my shit, digging her claws in.

But it's crazy to think that.

"Get a grip," I mutter, because Natalie would never screw me over. She's not like those others. She's not a kick-'em-in-the-balls kind of woman.

Except . . . you've only known her six months, dude.

I scrub my skin harder and try to talk myself off the ledge. I'm being ridiculous. Natalie and I spent *one* night together, and she already organized the annulment to fix our mistake. Just because I've got a couple of nutso chicks behind me doesn't mean the chick I nailed last night will go cuckoo, too.

But, calling her *the chick I nailed* seems wrong, especially as the metal on my finger glints at me, reminding me of how much more than *nailing* it was with her. Bits and pieces of laughter and lightness jostle in my brain, along with a memory of sweet, tender kisses, of a connection that felt deeper.

I didn't just nail her last night. I'm sure of it. What happened between the two of us was way more than that.

I'm equally sure it can't happen again.

CHAPTER SIXTEEN

Thirty minutes later, my shades are on, my headache has dialed down to dull, thanks to the aspirin, and I slide into a cool, air-conditioned car that takes us to a strip mall. We don't talk the entire ride. I don't even know what to say. She doesn't seem to want to engage, either. Maybe I pissed her off with my *tricked me* comment. Or maybe she's just got a mother of hangover headaches, too.

We park in front of Easy Out Divorce.

A thirty-something man with a diamond earring and a striped purple shirt strides out to greet us. He shakes hands gregariously, ushers us into his bare-bones office with a metal desk, and walks us through the process with a cheerful demeanor.

"And that's all you need to do," he says, flashing a smile. "It'll be $199 for the preparation of the paperwork, and then you'd need to file it at the courthouse yourself, and the filing fee is $269. You can do that on Monday. We'll give you instructions."

Natalie shakes her head. "We need the full-service package. We're flying back now."

He snaps his fingers, awareness dawning. "Right, right. We talked about that on the phone this morning. You're the New Yorkers." He claps his big hands together. "We'll need to kick this up a notch and do it all for you. We'll prep the joint annulment, file it, and pay the court fees." He makes a swooping gesture with his hand. "Then, we pick up the annulment decree signed by the judge." Now, he mimes signing a paper. "And all that is only $799. You can pay a deposit and make payments, or pay it all now. What sounds good to you?"

"Payments," Natalie says at the same time as I declare, "Pay it all now."

The dude's eyes widen, and he holds up his hands as if to say *keep me out of this.*

"I'd rather make payments," Natalie says in a quiet but firm voice.

"I got this." I grab my credit card from my wallet.

She grits her teeth then speaks in a low hiss to me, "I think we can both pay the cost of the annulment, Wyatt."

"No need. I'll take care of it."

"I want to split the fee." Each word from her is a bite. "And if we keep fighting about this, it's going to make my headache return."

Ditto, so I'm not going to belabor this point. Nor I am going to give in to her "let's go Dutch on a divorce" stance. "We just need to get it done, Nat. Stop arguing, and we can deal with it later."

She crosses her arms as I hand the guy my card and tell him, "The whole shebang."

He takes the payment, tells us where to sign on the dotted line, and says he'll keep us posted. "Congratulations on getting un-married," he says with a smile and a wave.

As we leave, Natalie gives me a stare. "What was that all about? Why do you get to pay for it?"

"Because it was *my* mistake."

"Ah. Right. Of course." She lingers on those words then shoots me a steely stare. "So back in the hotel, I might have tricked you? But now it's *your* mistake?" I start to answer, but she gives me no room to speak as she moves closer, getting in my face. "Maybe I wanted to pay to undo it, too. You're not the only one who made a mistake."

"That's not what I meant," I say as I open the door for her.

"Well, what *did* you mean?"

"Look," I say as I follow her into the car and the driver pulls out, "I'm sorry. I'm sorry things got crazy last night. I'm sorry I suggested we get married. I'm sorry the whole night was a mess. I'm sorry for everything. The least I can do is pay for it, though."

She closes her eyes like this pains her. "Now, I'm really sorry." Her voice is quiet, defeated.

I've no clue how we went from having the night of our lives to bickering like an old married couple. Oh, right. We got married. That's how. We did something unbearably stupid. But at least we can unravel that big mistake. "Look, the sooner this is over the better, right?"

"Absolutely."

"And it'll be over soon. Like the guy said." As the car rolls along the highway, I try to lighten the mood. "Hey, I guess the saying really is true. What happens in Vegas, stays in Vegas. We'll go back to New York with a clean slate. It'll be just like last night never happened."

"It sure will," she says through tight lips as she turns to stare out the window for the rest of the ride.

WELL HUNG · 123

We don't say much on the flight home. Or on the drive into Manhattan. When we reach her apartment, I clear my throat.

But what am I supposed to say? *Thanks for the lovely memories of a beautiful night I'll never forget?*

I can't say that, though. Things are strained between us, but it's for the best because we can't be together.

Instead, I use my best professional voice. "See you at the office."

She gives a cursory wave good-bye, and I head home and sleep off the rest of my bad decisions until Monday morning comes and I have to face her again.

CHAPTER SEVENTEEN

By now it should be apparent that I don't always make the best choices with women. Not sure why. Maybe I have a sign on my forehead that says, "Crazy? Consider me. I pair well with insane women. Like a good wine and cheese."

I don't blame the women because I'm a man who takes responsibility for his shit. I know I'm the one with the problem, and it started with Roxy. She caught my eye during my senior-year astronomy elective. We moved in together after college, and she worked late hours in public relations at a big New York firm. I burned the midnight oil, too, trying to earn my stripes as a master carpenter. Roxy was great, totally supportive, and everything a young guy working his way up in Manhattan could want—fun, supportive, and upbeat, as well as wild in the sack. But that's not the point. The point is she's the one who urged me to strike out on my own and build my carpentry business. She even provided some tips and guidance on incorporating.

Can you tell where this is going?

Yeah, so can I.

She was instrumental in encouraging me to start my shop, but after she spread her legs for the banker, I encouraged her to spread her wings from my life and get the fuck out of my apartment.

She packed up and shacked up with him. Too bad that wasn't the last of her. A month later, she tried to dig her claws into my business, claiming in her legal motion that she provided the "intellectual capital" to help me get started. That her late nights plotting and planning with me meant she deserved a piece of WH Carpentry & Construction. All that cheerleading had to have earned her something, she claimed.

She wanted a percentage of the revenue in perpetuity, and she was ready to fight me for it.

It was a mess, and my buddy Chase put me in touch with his cousin, who's a total shark of a lawyer. He helped me out, and I owe them both big time.

I wish I could see this kind of thing coming. I wish I knew when I was going to get involved with someone who'd try to kick me in the balls of my business. I've wondered if I am too trusting, but honestly, I don't think that's the issue. I'm not a fall-first-ask-questions-later kind of guy.

Take Katrina. I was careful with her, waited till our website contract ended. I changed the passwords just as a precautionary measure before I asked her out. She seemed liked a sweetheart, and even my sister liked her. And, hell, it isn't easy getting the Josie Hammer seal of approval.

Suffice to say, we were all shocked when Katrina went off the rails.

Josie declared it was just my particular brand of bad luck. Besides, everyone has that one friend who dates the crazies. Guess I fill that quota for all my buds. But it's not like there's a litmus test for crazy. That's yet another reason why I need to stay far away from the temptation Natalie brings to work.

Although my assistant looks perfectly delectable on Monday morning, sitting at her desk doing paperwork, I don't let my mind linger on her bare legs or her long neck. Nor do I cop a peek at those absolutely fantastic tits that she loves having bitten. And I certainly don't spend another second picturing her hitching her legs over my ass and digging her nails into my flesh.

My mind is clean as a whistle, because I cashed out ahead this weekend in Vegas, getting that annulment filed in the nick of time. I hope it means my bad luck streak is ending, and I'm safe and secure on the other side of trouble. Judging from the bright smile plastered on Natalie's face, she's perfectly content to be moving on, too. Like it didn't even happen.

"Good news. We got a call for an estimate on a kitchen redo on Park Avenue," she says then rattles off the details and tells me I'm needed there at four.

I fiddle with a box of paperclips on her desk. "Great. Will you do the schematics?"

"Of course. That's my job."

As I grab my tools and make my way out, I say goodbye, and she gives a quick wave. I do a double take when I see her left hand. Her fingers are bare. Her ring is gone.

Mine's still on, and I'm honestly not sure why I didn't take it off when I returned, or even notice I was still wearing it.

A momentary pang of sadness settles briefly into my chest, but that's pointless so I shove the feeling away and focus on work for the next several hours.

Later that day, Natalie joins me at the appointment, her laptop case in hand. She's professional to a T, answers the client's questions, and makes me look like a rock star.

On the way out of the building, I thank her then ask how she's doing today. "Everything good with you?"

She taps her wrist. "Everything's great, but I need to run. Karate class. Bye."

In a minute, she fades from my sight, turning north onto Park and blending into the sea of New Yorkers. Still ringless.

Back at my apartment, I toy with the band. I run my thumb and forefinger over the metal, but I don't yet take it off.

As I whip up an omelet for dinner, I wonder how Natalie prefers her eggs, whether she'd like my omelets. As I sit down and dig in, I slide the ring off and spin it absently in circles on the kitchen table.

When I'm done eating, I pop an Oreo in my mouth and click open my e-reader to my latest book of fascinating facts. As I read, I let the ring fall from one finger to the next, back and forth, back and forth. I set down my e-reader and wander into my bedroom, picking up the cardboard-framed photo of the two of us on the top of the rollercoaster. But looking at it makes me long for what I can't have, so I set it down.

Later, I hold the wedding band under the bathroom light then drop it in the medicine cabinet, wondering what Natalie did with hers.

* * *

But it doesn't matter, because a week later when I call Easy Out Divorce, the garrulous guy tells me, "It's all in process. The paperwork was filed. You'll be a free man in no time."

"Great," I say.

And it is great. It's truly great how quickly you can undo a massive mistake. I tell Natalie when I stop by the office on the way home from the new job we booked last week.

Her cool smile, along with a quick "great news," is her only answer. She gathers her purse, shoves it on her shoulder, and takes off.

That's how we continue for the next two weeks. We go out on estimates; we plan new projects. I build; she manages. We book a few new jobs, including one for a friend of Lila's. Her name is Violet, and she tells us she was so inspired by Lila's new kitchen that she wants a similar look and feel. I give Natalie a big thumbs-up when she shows me the contract for that gig, since it'll put us back on the expansion path.

"We'll start on it in a few more weeks. We have an opening then to fit this in," Natalie says in a professional voice. "And Lila seemed happy to connect us with Violet. She said when she came to my self-defense class again how awful she felt about the Vegas job falling through."

"She went to one of your classes?"

Natalie nods. "Yes. Funny thing. I was so used to seeing her in the context of working with you, and then all of a sudden there she was. She said she wants to learn self-defense."

"That's pretty cool."

"She's a quick learner. And I'm thrilled she told a friend about you. This pretty much gets us back on track after the Vegas debacle."

At first I'm not sure which debacle she's referring to— the marriage or the job cancellation—but then I realize she means the business. And that's fine with me, since we're showing how well we work together as soon-to-be an-nulees. We're all professional, all cool, unruffled feathers. As if we're proving with every goddamn interaction how completely unaffected we are by that night in Vegas.

Why should we act otherwise? After all, we went into that evening planning to make the most of it, and we did what we intended. We enjoyed the full Vegas experience, and we left it all behind when the sun came up.

Tonight, I'm going to keep forgetting about it since I'm off to a Yankees game. First, I stop by Sunshine Bakery, where Josie is closing up. She sweeps the floor as I enter and beams when she sees me.

I smile, too. "You didn't forget, did you?"

She laughs and shakes her head. "You only told me five times."

I hold up a finger. "*Once.* I told you once. Because I told Chase I'd tell you once. It's embarrassing enough."

"You must really owe him big time, then."

"He's collecting from years ago."

Josie sets the broom against the wall and heads behind the counter. She grabs a small yellow bakery box. A heart sticker is affixed on the box to keep it closed. She thrusts it at me. "One strawberry shortcake cupcake for Chase Summers."

"Can't believe I'm bringing a fucking cupcake all the

way to the Bronx for that bastard." I sniff the box. "Please tell me there's a seven-layer bar in here for me as a reward?"

"No such luck." She points to the heart sticker. "It's only for him."

I read her writing: *The manliest cupcake in the world. Not :) But glad you enjoy it, and glad you missed it. Come visit soon! It's been too long!*

"I swear, Josie. It was all he talked about when we made plans. *Are you bringing me a cupcake? Are you bringing me a cupcake?* I was like, *Dude, get your own.* But he's had day-time shifts all week, so hasn't been able to make it. And I had to take pity on him seeing as how, well, you know . . ." I make a rolling gesture with my hand.

"He saved lives in war-torn Africa for the last year," Josie supplies. "The man deserves a cupcake. Be sure to tell Doctor McHottie to stop by to get another one."

I shoot her a look. "Don't call him that."

Her eyes widen in a *who me* expression. "That's what you used to call him."

I shake my head. "Trust me. I never called him that."

"Then who did?"

"All. The. Ladies."

She gestures to herself. "I'm a lady."

"And he's a dog."

She laughs. "Sounds like a compliment, then, since you like dogs."

I consider that briefly. "Got me on that one," I say, then make my way to the door. But I stop halfway and rap my knuckles on a yellow table as I consider whether I'm missing a chance to pry. I mean, check in on Natalie. "Hey, Josie," I say, all nonchalant.

"Yeah?"

"Everything good with Natalie?"

Josie tilts her head to the side. "Of course. Why do you ask?"

I shrug. "No reason. Just making sure."

Josie stares at me, and I know I've said too much. This is my sister, and she reads emotions as if they're tattooed on your forehead. "Did something go wrong in Vegas?"

I scoff. "No. God no," I say, giving a champion-level denial. Then, worry strikes. "Why? Did she mention anything?"

"No. I just was curious. She's been a little quieter lately, though. Did you say something stupid to her?"

About a million stupid things.

"No more than usual," I say with a cheesy grin, breathing a sigh of relief.

"Seriously, though. Were you a good guy?" she says, her big green eyes pinning me. Challenging me. Making me ask myself the same question. Does marrying Natalie on a whim and annulling it let me stay in the good guy camp? Running through the time in Vegas with Natalie, I decide I was a good guy. Maybe not a bright guy. Maybe not a cautious guy. But at least I treated her well, and I've been a good boss since we returned.

"I was very good. So good I deserve a seven-layer bar," I say, batting my eyes.

She laughs and grabs a bar from behind the counter. "You know I always give you one."

"You're the best sister in the entire world, world, world," I call out, making my voice echo, as if I'm talking in a microphone.

"I know, I know, I know. Give Chase a hug for me."

"Never. That will never happen."

CHAPTER EIGHTEEN

At Yankee Stadium, I find my college buddy in the third row by the first baseline, tapping away on his phone. "Yo. All the women swiping left on you?" I clap him on the back. "It's rough being everyone's last choice in Tinder."

"Don't you know it, man," he says, then knocks fists with me. "Good to see you."

"You, too." I eye his skin, a golden-brown hue now. "Guess a year working outside will do this to you."

He holds out one arm. "Like my tan? I really am the golden boy now," he says, then winks and grabs for the cupcake box. "C'mon. I missed my sweets when I was gone."

Chase just returned from a year working with Doctors Without Borders. He served shortly after he finished his residency in ER medicine, and now he's back in New York, working at a trauma hospital.

"No cupcakes in Africa?"

"Shockingly, no," he says, as he reads the sticker, smiles, and opens the box. He pops a chunk of the strawberry treat in his mouth. He rolls his eyes in pleasure and points. "This is the meaning of life. Right here. This cupcake."

"Josie is pretty much a goddess of baked goods."

"She is," he says, adoration thick in his tone. "And this just makes my whole day better. Trust me, it was a shit afternoon. Well, for other people."

"Let me guess. You had five stabbings," I say, as a recap of last night's game-winning homer plays on the Jumbotron.

He runs a hand through his—you guessed it—golden-brown hair and laughs deeply. "Four, actually. Along with three gunshots and a mustard jar inside a body cavity," he says, then tells me exactly where the jar was found while he devours the pink frosting.

I cringe. "Dude, how can you eat while you tell that story?"

He shrugs. "I was born lacking any semblance of squeamishness. Guess that's one reason I'm so amazing at my job," he deadpans, like the cocky fucker I've known him to be. He's a great guy, though. He's always had my back, and I'm the same with him.

He finishes the cupcake, tucks the sticker in his pocket, and says, "Tell Josie she's still the best baker around."

"You should go in. Tell her yourself," I say, since Josie and Chase know each other. He came home for a few breaks during college and stayed with us, and they became friendly. I stop, remembering the McHottie comment. "Wait. Don't go in. Don't see her."

He frowns and holds up his hands as if weighing something. "See her, don't see her? Which one is it, Hammer?"

"See her, Summers. But don't hit on her," I warn.

His eyebrows wriggle. "She's still a total babe, right?"

I scowl. "Dude. Don't say that. She's my sister, not to mention my favorite person in the universe."

"Empirically, though, she's gorgeous. It's a medical fact."

"You can't just say that shit on account of the degree. You can't. It's not allowed," I say as the Yankees stream out of the dugout and the crowd cheers.

"Relax, man. I've been friends with her nearly as long as I've been friends with you. And I haven't hit on her once."

"Good. Can we talk about something else besides my sister?"

"Sure," he says, casually. "Like, say, how's life as a married man?"

I jerk my head. Glance down at my ring finger. It's bare. "How'd you know?"

He laughs deeply. "Dude, you texted me at three in the morning from Vegas and said you got hitched. I thought you were pranking me. It was for real?" he asks as the announcer shares the lineup, and the players' names and pictures flash on the Jumbotron.

I shrug, nod, and say yes.

"What's the story?"

I give him the CliffsNotes version of what an amazing time Natalie and I had in Vegas, then buy a couple of brews from the beer man in the stands. And since I haven't breathed a word to anyone, it actually feels good to tell Chase what went down.

"So you still haven't fixed that little issue?" he asks as I hand him a cup. "I told you, there's a pill for that. You should have taken it that night."

"What's the name of this pill?" I ask, taking the bait.

He taps his chin. "Let's see. What was the name of it? A pharma rep brought one by the other day. Oh, right. It's called Do the Motherfucking Opposite of Every Instinct You Have When it Comes to Women."

"So it's an opposite pill you're prescribing after the fact."

"Seriously, though, man," he says, clasping my shoulder. "It's a no harm, no foul situation. You've got it all sorted out, and now you move on."

"Yeah, totally," I say, taking a drink, but the words feel strangely empty.

"Hell, everyone does stupid shit in Vegas."

"It's the land of stupid shit."

"It's like a rite of passage."

"Except you. You never do stupid shit," I point out, and it's true. Chase is the golden boy through and through. He skipped two grades in school, scored a full scholarship to college, and graduated top of his class. Went on to medical school, nabbed a great residency, then decided to take a year to help out in one of the most war-torn regions in the world. Oh, and he can save lives. So, there's that. He has absolutely no problems when it comes to the ladies.

"No, I don't. But if I were in Vegas, I'd probably have done the same," he says. "Especially if I had a thing for my assistant like you do."

I whip my head in his direction even though the bases are now loaded. "What? Why the fuck do you say that? You've only been back in town for two weeks. How would you know?"

He raises an eyebrow. "Methinks the gentleman doth protest too much."

"Whatever. Answer the question, man."

Chase takes a hearty drink of the beer. "Because of how you just talked about her. You like this woman."

I part my lips to speak, but what's there to say? He's right. I do like Natalie. I have from day one. But that doesn't matter. My feelings aren't the issue. The situation, however, is the issue, and it's not changing anytime soon.

"Besides," he continues, "you're not the type of dude who just hits 'em and quits 'em."

"I have a Tinder account," I say defensively as the pitcher serves up a strike.

"And you've used it, what, once?"

I shrug sheepishly. He's right. Tinder isn't my thing. "Once. Yeah."

"Good luck, then, working with her every day. That's got to really suck."

Another strike flies over the plate. "Thanks. Thanks a lot. This pep talk was awesome. Now I'm fired up for the nine-to-five grind."

"Life could be worse," he says, with an evil grin. "You could be in the ER with a mustard jar up your butt."

CHAPTER NINETEEN

On the scale of suckage, working with Natalie isn't as bad as, say, smacking your thumb with a hammer. Nor does it bite as hard as whacking your knee on the entertainment center you just installed in a newly renovated Tribeca loft for a famous director, and his superstar actress wife.

Sure, smacks and whacks are an occupational hazard, but the last time I nailed myself twice in one day . . . wait, that sounds really dirty. Anyway, suffice to say, the ice age I'm *not* enjoying with Natalie is throwing me off my game at work. But I do my best to shove all thoughts of her from my mind so I can finish the Tribeca job.

It's not easy. Natalie seems to occupy an annoyingly large portion of my mental real estate these days, and I'd like to evict her.

At the very least, I'd like to relocate her to the *just co-workers* portion of my brain.

When I return to the office to drop off the tools, Natalie is chatting on the phone. "Perfect. I'll be there tonight.

Sixty-Fourth and Lex. I really appreciate you thinking of me for the extra class."

I raise an eyebrow and give her a thumbs-up. Call me Encyclopedia Brown, but I'm guessing she scored another karate gig. When she hangs up, I hold my arms out wide. "Kicking ass and taking names?"

She smiles, and all is right with the world. In her grin, I can feel the tension that's been strung between us since Vegas seep away. We're back to who we were before. We're the coworkers who support each other. We're the colleagues who eat spicy food together. We're all good. "Yes. Another dojo has me on its substitute list. I'm thrilled."

I narrow my brow. "Substitute list? You should be doing your own classes."

She shrugs. "It's fine. It works for me."

"But how is that helping you with your videos and building your rep as a teacher? People should want to come to *your* classes, not stumble upon you when you're filling in for some schmo who can't make his own session."

"It works for me, Wyatt," she says crisply, and maybe I'm not back in her good graces after all.

"I just think you're selling yourself short."

"Don't worry about it. Really, I'm fine." She taps the pile of checks on her desk. "Some bills are due. I filled out the checks. If you could just sign them, I can get them in the mail on my way out."

She hands me a pen, and I feel like I've been scolded and sent to bed without supper. Maybe I spoke out of line. I can't read her anymore. I bend lower to sign, and I'm so close I can smell her. I swallow dryly, remembering what it was like to run my nose along her hair, to drag my lips over her skin, to breathe her in. I curse myself for never going down on her that night. What was I thinking? My mouth waters as I sign the checks and dream about kneeling under the desk between her legs and burying my face under that skirt. Tasting her sweet heat. Licking her, sucking her, lapping her up.

"Fuck," I mutter.

"What's wrong?"

My dick is an iron spike and my brain is a carousel of images of your supremely tantalizing naked body, that's what's wrong. But we can solve it easily if you'd spread your legs and let me eat you out right the fuck now.

"Nothing's wrong. All good." I wave a hand dismissively, and try to position myself so my hard-on isn't visible. A memory flickers, of Natalie telling me on the pinball machine that she used to check me out at work. I wonder if she still does. If her eyes are on my crotch once more, and if she's pleased with the effect she's had. If she'd like to do anything to ease the ache I feel right now. And most of all I wonder if she feels the same.

"Last check," she says, sliding the final one in front of me, her hands dangerously near to my dick. "It's my paycheck."

I lift the pen over the signature line and begin to give it my John Hancock, when I flinch. The amount is wrong.

"What's that?" I point to the check. I'm not thinking about what's between her legs anymore. I'm thinking about what she's doing with my business.

"We call it a check. It's like a promise for money. You take it to the bank and they give you cash in that amount," she says, and her tone is half-playful, like maybe we've gone back to getting along.

But my question wasn't so fundamental. "I meant, why is *that* the amount? It's wrong," I say, tapping the black ink she filled in earlier.

"That's my normal pay."

I heave a sigh as an unfamiliar anger courses through me. I'm not a guy with a temper. I don't get pissed off. But if she's doing what I think she's doing, this makes me fucking mad. "I gave you a raise, Natalie." My voice is strung tight. "Did you forget?"

She lifts her face. Her eyes look guilty, but her words seem certain. "I didn't forget. I just figured it no longer applied."

I press my hands onto her desk and stare her down. "We annulled the marriage, not the employment."

"I just thought it was one of those things."

"One of what things?"

"One of those things you say when you're drunk," she fires back.

I grit my teeth and breathe in hard through my nostrils. "But yet I meant it."

She pushes back in her chair. "Look, I didn't want to be presumptuous and assume the raise still applied. I didn't want to put you in a position where you felt *obligated*," she says, enunciating that last word with precision, and it almost feels as if she's throwing it back at me for some reason.

And that pisses me off even more. These last few weeks have been nothing but us tiptoeing around each other, and now here she is making motherfucking decisions for my business that she's not authorized to make.

"This is my company. I decide what to pay you." I don't raise my voice. She gets my meaning by the coldness of my tone, and the way I hold up the check and rip it down the middle.

I grab a new one and write the correct amount. A bigger amount. I hand it to her. "I told you I was giving you a ten percent raise, and I meant it. I made you a promise, and I goddamn intend to stick to it, whether I had a few beers or not. I'm a man of my word, and I sure as hell expect the people I work with to treat me like it and to act the same way."

"Thank you." With shaky hands, she takes the check, lowers her face, grabs her purse, and scurries far away from me. I sink down in her chair, anger seething through me, and I drop my head in my hands.

"Fuck, fuck, fuck."

I shouldn't be so pissed. I know that. But tell that to the fury that's racing through me right now. I *hate* feeling like this. I pride myself on being a laidback guy, and I'm the opposite of that now. I head home, change into shorts, and work out in the gym in my building, lifting more weight than I should, running faster than I usually do, and generally pushing myself into stupid-guy zone, because I'm pissed.

And I hardly know why.

But after a hot shower at home, the knotted up thoughts begin to untangle. Soon enough, I know why I'm mad.

It's not because she tried to subvert me by paying herself *less*. That's ridiculous.

It's not because we were drunk and pieces of the night are still a haze to me. It's because we're not the same. We didn't go back to being Natalie and Wyatt. We went into full-on boss-assistant mode, and I liked it much better when we had a good time together at work, before work became as pleasant as a root canal.

I pull on jeans and a T-shirt, drag my fingers through my mostly dry hair, and leave my building. I hoof it across town and hope to hell she's still at the dojo on Sixty-Fourth. As the clock ticks toward nine, the lights from the studio shine brightly, and I spot Natalie inside, closing the place. Jamming my thumbs into the pockets of my jeans, I wait.

A few minutes later, the lights flicker and turn off. The door opens, and Natalie locks it then turns around.

"Oh." Her eyes widen.

"Hey," I say softly.

"Hey." Her tone matches mine, and that instant gentleness is like a caress.

"I was an ass. I'm sorry."

She smiles. "It's all right. I shouldn't have—"

I cut her off. This one is on me. "No. I would have done the same if I were you. I should never have put you in the position of doubting what I would pay you. Is that why you took the substitute job? Because you weren't sure if the raise was real?"

She nods guiltily. "I needed the extra money."

My heart falls. "I'm sorry, Nat. I mean it. I don't want you to doubt your value, or my words, or what I promise you. I need to do better. I want to do better. And I want to pay you what you deserve for the amazing job you do."

"Thank you."

"I couldn't run the business without you. That's why you got a raise. No other reason."

"Thank you. I really appreciate that."

"You really deserve it." I take a beat. "So are we good?"

"We're good," she says, and for the first time since I woke up with a hangover, I feel like that might be true.

Her stomach rumbles, and I smile. "I think you might want something else, though. Dinner? I'm buying. Burgers and beer?"

The grin that stretches across her face is the first one since we returned from Vegas that feels like her. Like the woman I've known. "I'm in."

The smile reassures me, too—tells me that sliding back into who we were before is going to be so damn easy.

I just know it.

CHAPTER TWENTY

Natalie points to my chin. "Ketchup," she says. I grab the napkin and wipe it off, then finish my story.

"Then, there was the time we took her copy of *Gone With the Wind*, cut out the last ten pages, and wrote *Rhett leaves. He's a dick.*"

She smacks my thigh. "You were so cruel."

I nod in agreement as I take a swig of my beer. We're seated at the counter at The Best Burger Joint in the City on Lexington as we work our way through the jalapeño hot sauce burger bites. "We were the worst. Josie had been dying to read it. She went through a Scarlett O'Hara phase and dressed up as a southern belle for Halloween, complete with a parasol."

"Oh, that's adorable. I'll have to ask if she still has pictures. But you and Nick were terrible. Cutting it up then spoiling the story." She shakes her head in amusement as she digs into a mini burger drenched in chili peppers.

"My mom sometimes said she thought we were identical, not fraternal, twins since we both were possessed by evil prankster DNA. Anyway, Josie was devastated. She went to our mom and asked, 'Is this true?' My mom marched into our bedroom, thrust the book at both of us, and said we were required to use our allowances and purchase not only a new copy, but any other books Josie wanted that year."

Natalie beams. "Excellent punishment. I guess Josie won that one after all."

"She did. Ask her what funded her Jane Austen collection, and it was us being little assholes." I take a bite of a burger. A Spoon song blasts overhead. As I finish chewing, I point upward. "Now this, this is music. Not that Katy Perry, Justin Bieber, Taylor Swift stuff you like."

She bumps my shoulder. "Katy Perry rocks. Taylor Swift is awesome. And don't even pretend I like the Biebs. I have standards, you musical snob."

"Thank god," I say under my breath, teasing her.

"But I still want to know—did Josie ever get back at you for spoiling the book?"

I nod. "Sure did. She exacted her revenge in other ways."

Natalie lifts her beer bottle and tips it back. "Tell me, tell me, tell me."

"She doused all our T-shirts in some girlie perfume one morning our freshman year of high school. There was nothing else to wear. We went to school like that."

Natalie pumps a fist. "Excellent. I'll congratulate her myself when I see her later. Leaving you and Nick smelling like princesses is the definition of sweet revenge."

"I smelled quite pretty," I say in a prissy voice, and that cracks her up. Then my tone darkens. "But I couldn't stop pranking her. I was a total dick."

She frowns. "No. Really?"

I nod, 'fessing up to my misdeeds. "I replaced her shampoo with vegetable oil."

Natalie's eyes widen. "You were Satan."

"The devil incarnate. I made fun of her the next day, too. Couldn't let it go. Told her she smelled like a greasy salad, which is a simple but awful thing to say to a twelve-year-old girl."

"Wyatt," she chides, her blue eyes shaming me. "That's terrible."

I hold up my hands in surrender. "I know. Trust me, I know. She was so upset, but she tried hard not to let on," I say, remembering how Josie's lip quivered and she hid in her room, trying to figure out why her hair was such an oily mess. "I couldn't even blame Nick because he was at a friend's house. My mom pulled me aside that night."

Natalie reaches for a fry on my plate and drags it through the hot sauce. She pops it into her mouth without flinching, and once again I'm impressed with her heat tolerance. "Were you in trouble?"

I sigh deeply, remembering the brilliance of my mother's punishment. "In a way. I wasn't grounded, but I got a talking to in front of a girl. I was fifteen and had my first real girlfriend, and she was over watching a movie with me. My mom came into the living room, turned off the TV, and explained what had happened, right in front of the girl I liked."

Natalie's jaw drops. "What did she say?"

"My girlfriend was pissed at me, and she agreed with my mom. My mom said how a boy treats his sister matters for many reasons, not the least because it'll teach her what to expect from boys and men. She said, 'Treat her with love, kindness, and respect, and set a good example for her. If you and Nick do that, she'll keep growing up to be a strong, confident woman who won't let a man walk all over her.'"

Natalie smiles softly. "I don't have a brother, but I do think that's true. I think we are all role models for each other."

"We are, right? Maybe it's the psych major in me, but I have a theory that we learn how we want to be treated and can expect to be treated not just from our parents, but our sisters and our brothers, too. It all matters. Everything we do matters."

Her lips twitch in a grin. "You were a psych major?"

I laugh. "Weird, right?" I hold up my hands. "Did you think I majored in woodshop?"

She shakes her head. "No, but come to think of it, psych sort of fits you."

"Yeah? How so?"

"You act like everything is so simple, but deep down you're more insightful than you let on. Most of the time." She winks. "Did your mom's talking-to work right away?"

"It did. I needed to straighten up. Treat her better. Stop the jokes and needless put-downs. And my mom really put it in perspective. Saying all that in front of a girl I liked just emphasized her point. My goal from then on was to be a good guy, and show Josie how a dude could be, and what she deserved."

"And look at her now," says Natalie. "She's strong, independent, and incredibly kind. She's also no doormat, so it looks like you did have a lasting impact on her by changing your behavior." Natalie wipes her hand on the napkin then rubs my shoulder as she talks. It occurs to me that this woman is tactile. She likes to touch. She likes to put her hands on me. She's always done it, and she's that way once again. I'm not entirely sure why this makes me happy, beyond the obvious—I really fucking enjoy her hands on me. But maybe also because it's a sign that we're back to normal. That the Vegas fallout is finished.

"That's what a brother should do. Show his sister she deserves the world. Let her know she should expect the best," I say, a burst of pride in my chest. "I might have been a wiseass, but because of the greasy salad hair, I worked harder to become a better guy. A good guy. She's the reason it's so damn important to me to be that kind of man."

Natalie takes a deep breath. For a moment, her eyes seem wet, almost as if she's holding back tears. She doesn't shed any, though, so maybe it's the spice. "Hot chili pepper?" I ask.

She nods and grabs a glass of ice water, gulping some down. But she doesn't say anything more, so I keep the conversation going with a question. "Is it weird to hear this since you live with her?"

She shakes her head. "No. I think it's wonderful." She turns to me, her eyes meeting mine, the look in them genuine. "I love her, and I love knowing how much you care about her."

Her voice does something to me. Warms me up. Squeezes my heart. "What about Charlotte? You're super close now. Did you always get along?"

She makes a "so-so" gesture then answers. "Most of the time, but when we were younger we fought like any siblings. I'd want to wear one of her skirts. She wouldn't want me to. That sort of thing." Natalie lowers her voice to a whispered confession, "I pranked her, too."

"You naughty girl." I wiggle my fingers, a sign for her to spill the beans. "What'd you do?"

"She was crazy focused in school, so one morning I set her alarm clocks wrong. Boy, was she pissed. She nearly missed a test. She was not happy with me. But it didn't matter, because I was so jealous of her."

I tilt my head. "Why?"

"School came easily to her. She breezed through high school and got into Yale like it was the easiest thing in the world." She turns away to fiddle with her beer bottle.

"And you? School wasn't your thing?"

"I was more interested in the physical stuff. I spent so much time and energy on martial arts, you know? But it still made me batty because school mattered more to my parents, and that's what she aced. I guess they were right, though. She runs a profitable business, and I'm just subbing in karate classes," she says, brushing her hair off her shoulder.

"Hey," I say, my voice soft. "You're not just a substitute. You're building yourself up. You're growing your reputation. And I have complete faith your video series is going to be amazing. Speaking of, are you going to show them to me?"

"Let me finish the edit, then I can email them to you," she suggests, a hopeful note in her voice. "If you really want to see them."

"I do. I'd love to see them and help you in any way I can."

Her eyes light up. "I'd really love some feedback."

"Count on it. I'll help you make them amazing. And hey, I also happen to think you're amazing at WH Carpentry & Construction. You're much more than an assistant, Nat. You manage the shop. You make it run."

And now her smile spreads wide across her face. "Really?"

She sounds so damn happy at the compliment, and her reaction thrills me. "You're awesome at what you do. You're invaluable."

"It's fun. I sort of feel like every day is this puzzle, and I get to make all the pieces fit."

"The WH jigsaw is better than being a phone sex manager?" I tease.

"*Much* better than furries and feet," she says with a laugh. She turns more serious, placing her hand on my forearm. "I truly enjoy my job, Wyatt, so I don't want you to think I'm looking to ditch this gig for karate teaching. I like making both work and martial arts fit in my life."

I wipe a hand across my brow. "Whew. Because you know I'd be a mess without you."

"I'm not planning on going anywhere. So long as you'll have me," she says. Then she seems to realize the double meaning and quickly corrects herself. "As long as you're happy with my work."

"I'm very happy with your work." I pick up my beer when I realize she never finished her story. "You didn't tell me what your punishment was for the alarm clocks."

"I had to do her laundry and dishes for a week."

I crack up. "Bet you never did that again."

Natalie shrugs happily. "It wasn't a punishment. I like laundry."

"No one likes laundry."

"I'm the exception, then. I like clean spaces. I like an organized home. I don't mind the work getting it there."

"You are quite the planner. I was impressed you brought condoms to Vegas." I pick up another burger, but before I bite it, I realize what just came out of my mouth. "Um, can we pretend I didn't say that?"

She laughs. "Listen, we don't need to tiptoe around each other. We don't have to pretend it didn't happen, either. Let's just be glad we're moving on. We had our fun, we put it behind us, and we can still hang out like we did before, as coworkers."

She takes a burger bite from the plate and holds it up in a toast and we knock . . . burgers. "I'll toast to that for sure. As coworkers."

We power through the plate, then order one more, quenching the fire with beer and returning to who we were. But that's not entirely true. Because when I walk her home and stand under the green awning that leads into her building, reality slams into me once more.

Here's the thing—even if you agree to return to the pre-sex days, even if you have an amazing time just being together, when you stand in front of her building, and all you can think about is why you can't go upstairs with her and fuck her against the wall, then kiss her till she's writhing and wriggling and begging you to stay the night and do it all again, you realize that putting the genie back in the bottle is damn near impossible.

"So this is it," she says, and her voice is feathery.

I nod, shifting back and forth on the balls of my feet. "This is it."

I swallow, and my throat is dry. Parched even. I lick my lips. She parts hers slightly, and I'm pretty damn sure neither one of us is buzzed this time. We hardly drank tonight, but even so, we seem to sway closer. Maybe there's just an invisible pull between us, tugging us nearer to each other. We're on her sidewalk, outside her apartment, and yet I'm only truly aware of her. How the breeze blows a few soft blond strands by her face. How she clasps her hands together, as if she's trying to figure out what to do with them. How her breath ghosts over her lips.

Neither one of us makes a move.

Then, she hugs me. "I'm really glad we spent time together tonight," she whispers, her mouth near my ear. A shiver moves through me.

"Me, too," I say softly, but I don't let go. It feels too good to have her in my arms. Instead, I hold her tighter. I breathe her in. I might even clasp her more closely, and she lets me. She snuggles into me, and right here, it feels like we're damn ready to let that genie fly all the way free tonight.

A car honks. My cue to pull away. We say good-bye, and I tell myself tomorrow it'll get easier to be near her.

But tomorrow morning, things get way more complicated.

CHAPTER TWENTY-ONE

I dig my thumbs and forefingers into the corners of my eyelids. If I can press hard enough, perhaps what the woman on the other end of the phone is telling me will change. But no matter how many times I ask if she's sure, the three things she says remain the same: the Las Vegas courthouse has no record of our annulment. Easy Out Divorce never filed it. Easy Out Divorce closed up shop and took our money.

"But you should be sure to call the credit card company and get your $799 back," the helpful lady suggests, as if it's the money I care about.

"Great. I'll need it for another annulment," I say then slam the receiver down. Benefit of office phones? You can still get angry with them in a way you can't with cells. Awesome.

When I turn around, Natalie is standing in the doorway. Her eyes are wide with worry. "What did you just say?" Each word is stilted.

"They never filed. We were scammed." I sink into the dingy office chair, dragging a hand through my hair.

She grips the doorframe. "What do we do next?"

"I really don't know," I say, tension thick in my veins because everything had been going well again, and now it turns out what happened in Vegas didn't fucking stay in Vegas. It followed us. This marriage is like an infection that won't go away. Looks like my streak continues.

Her eyes swing toward the wall clock. "You better go, Wyatt. You don't want to be late for the job. Let's grab the cabinet doors and get you out of here. I'll take care of this today. I promise. I'll figure it out."

"Okay," I say with a sigh, and I'm glad she's on top of the work schedule because I already forgot where I was headed this morning.

She helps me gather the wood materials I need, hands them to me, then grabs my tool belt from the chair where I left it last night. Her eyes register that my hands are full, and before I even know it, hers are around my hips and she's buckling the tool belt in place.

"There," she declares then walks me to the truck in the parking garage I use next to our office.

"Hector's coming today to help you out. Just focus on work. Seriously, I've got this," she says, wrapping her soft hand around my arm like the Frisky Mittens she is. I blink away the thought. *Can't think of her like that.*

She hands me something wrapped in brown paper.

"What's this?"

"Just a way of saying thanks for last night. I made you a sandwich for your lunch. Extra sriracha. And an Oreo is in there, too. Your favorite," she says, with a sweet little smile, a gesture that tells me she wants me to like this.

I do like it. "Thank you," I say, and as I get into the truck and drive off, it hits me how wifely that whole exchange was. Fastening the tool belt. Seeing me to the vehicle. Handing me a lunch she made.

Just like she's Mrs. Hammer.

And she is.

But as I click on the blinker to turn onto 10th Avenue, an idea lands in my head out of nowhere. She's never made me a sandwich before. What if she spread arsenic in the sriracha? What if this is all her secret ploy as Mrs. Hammer to take over my business? She's the one who tracked down the annulment company. What if she knew it was a bogus service? What if she's tricking me so she can have everything of mine when I'm sleeping with the fishes thanks to this sandwich?

A cab slams its horn, blaring in my ears, and I slam on the brakes.

Holy shit. I nearly ran a red light. My pulse skitters out of control as I wait at the intersection.

Get it together, Hammer. No one is trying to kill you. You're being paranoid. You need to chill out.

I take several deep breaths, clear my mind, and focus on driving. After I park and head to the client's building, I toss the sandwich in the trash can on the corner.

Better safe than six feet under.

A few minutes later, from the fourth-floor window of today's job, I spot a homeless dude rooting around in the trash can, grabbing it.

Great. Now his dirt nap will be on my hands.

* * *

Natalie: What do I do now???

Charlotte: I called a friend who's a lawyer. She walked me through it. It's honestly not a big deal. There are basically two routes. The first is you could go redo the paperwork for Nevada and file by mail, but there's a chance a judge might want to see you in person for a hearing.

Natalie: What's the second?

Charlotte: The other option, and this is probably your safest bet just to make sure everything is done properly, is to get a divorce in NY.

Natalie: Ugh, I don't want to be divorced. I wanted to not be married.

Charlotte: I get it, but this seems like a decent solution. It's easy, too. In your case, you'd do what's called an uncontested divorce. And those are different than the long, protracted NY divorces we all hear about.

Natalie: Why can't we just get the marriage annulled in NY?

Charlotte: Well, let's see if you qualify. Were either one of you married to someone else?

Natalie: Um. No.

Charlotte: So no bigamy case can be made, then. Check that off. Were either of you unable to have sexual intercourse at the time of the marriage?

Natalie: Very funny. We were the opposite. Apparently that's all we were able to do.

Charlotte: I thought so :) And were either of you incurably insane for five or more years?

Natalie: Definitely for the entire night. Does that count?

Charlotte: Doesn't quite add up to five years, I'm afraid. So, as you can see, New York is a wee bit complicated when it comes to granting annulments. Weirdly, divorce is easier in NY. At least, an uncontested divorce is. I vote for that.

Natalie: Great. Now I'll be a divorced woman. It'll be this black mark.

Charlotte: They don't brand divorced people, Nat. Or make you get a tattoo.

Natalie: I know there's no shame in divorcing for real. But this isn't a real divorce. It's dumbass divorce, born from vodka, hormones, and stupidity. I was such an idiot.

Charlotte: You were just having fun.

Natalie: In my case, fun = idiocy

Charlotte: Stop beating yourself up. Just do what you need to do.

Natalie: I will . . . I'm just so . . . I can't focus . . . My videos suck . . . This whole situation is getting me down.

Charlotte: Why?

Natalie: You know why

Charlotte: Because of how you feel?

Natalie: I HATE FEELINGS. MAKE THEM STOP.

Charlotte: Poof. Done.

Natalie: I love you. Thank you. I'm better now.

Charlotte: Come over later, and we'll cuddle. For now, I'm emailing you all the details of what to do next.

* * *

At four o'clock, I cross the sidewalk to my truck, loading the tools in the cab. A dude with a scraggly beard and a filthy jacket wanders past me. He stops, turns around, and gives me a thumbs-up. "Hey, man, don't know why you threw out that sandwich this morning, but I'm glad you did. It was awesome."

My face is blank for a few seconds, then it dawns on me. He survived the turkey ambush. Which means not only did I *not* become an accessory to murder, Natalie didn't try to off me with a ciabatta.

Of course she didn't, you idiot. You jumped to conclusions. You assumed the worst. You lumped her in with all the others. You should have known better.

When I return to the office, she's placing the pages she just printed on her desk. I set down the tools, walk over to her, and park my hands on her shoulders.

She blinks, surprised I'm so close.

Chase's advice resonates.

Do the opposite.

CHAPTER TWENTY-TWO

If my instinct has been to assume she wanted me terminated via turkey, I'm going to do the opposite. "The sandwich was to die for," I tell her, privately enjoying my inside joke. I wrap my arms around her in a hug.

I can feel her smile against my shoulder. "It was just a sandwich, but you're welcome."

When we separate, our eyes meet, and my gratitude disappears. So does my stupidity. In its place is only desire. I brush her hair from her cheek, run my thumb along her jawline, and bring my forehead to hers. "I want you so fucking much," I tell her, because it's not only the truth—it's the opposite of what I wanted to say to her this morning.

She grips my shirt and her eyes darken. "I want you so much it drives me crazy."

A lusty sort of relief floods me. Cupping her cheeks in my hands, I gaze into her eyes, and the fire inside me intensifies. What flickered earlier is now blazing. I slant my mouth to hers, and the second our lips touch, all these warring emotions settle, replaced by only the absolute rightness of what I feel for her.

Her lips part, and I slide my tongue inside her mouth. My head spins, and my heart slams against my chest. I've missed this. I've craved this. I've needed this. I kiss her like there's nothing else in the world I'd rather do. My body aligns with her, my erection against her hip, and she moans lightly, pulling me closer as she backs up. Her ass hits the metal desk, then she scoots up on it. My eyes snap open to see papers sliding behind her, then to the floor. She perches on the desk, opening her legs to draw me against her.

I'm there, wedged between her thighs, my throbbing erection pressed hard against her skin. *Where it belongs.* Jesus Christ. This is where I want to be. Here with her. Ready for me.

I break the kiss, dragging my rough hands down her bare arms. She shudders as I touch her, and wraps her legs more tightly around me.

"I can't stop thinking about fucking you again, Nat. About touching you again," I say, bringing my mouth to her ear. "And tasting you."

She trembles as a soft gasp falls from her lips.

"You'd like that, wouldn't you?" I pull her earlobe between my teeth and nip the flesh. "I bet you'd like my face between your legs."

Her answer sounds wanton as she moans *yes.*

And that's how I find myself pushing her down on the desk, hiking up her knees so her high heels hook over the edge, and spreading those strong, toned legs. I push her skirt to her waist, tug her panties to the side, and then kiss her hot, wet pussy.

She tastes like heaven on my tongue, and a rumble works its way up my chest. She's so slick, and there's nothing better than knowing the woman you want is this hot for you. The caveman in me wants to go wild on her, to kiss her pussy in a relentless devouring. But I've got to get her there first. Can't just start at sixty miles an hour. I pace myself, flicking my tongue over the rise of her clit.

"Oh my God," she moans, and I smile as all the memories of her sexy sounds return. I love how loud she is, the noises she makes, the things she says. "I've been fantasizing . . . Your lips are just . . ." Her words are broken by her panting breaths, as I suck her clit into my mouth in a way that makes her writhe.

"Yeah? You've been wanting me to eat you?" I raise my face and grab her pink panties, pulling them off in one smooth motion.

"So much, so much," she says, lifting up her hips like a fucking invitation, like she needs this as desperately as I do.

I kiss the top of her mound then whisper, "Show me that it's all you've been thinking about."

I return to the glorious land between her legs. Her pussy glistens with her arousal, so wet and shiny that I half want to admire the sight of her slick pink flesh, but I wholly want to consume it and be consumed by her. Pressing my hands to her legs, I spread her open again and lick, a long, lush stroke all the way up, spearing my tongue against her throbbing clit at the top.

She cries out my name.

My tongue goes in reverse, trailing down.

She moans God's name.

And I go to town, lapping her wetness. Sucking her sweetness. Devouring her until she's panting and writhing and saying Jesus's name this time. Maybe I can get her to call out all the saints, too.

Her hands seek my hair, grabbing, clamping down. Her hips lift, matching my moves as I kiss her pussy the way I've kissed her lips. *Hungrily.* Like I can't get enough to eat.

"It's so good, it's so good, it's so good," she moans, tugging on my hair, pulling my face closer, even though, trust me, I'm buried in her right now. There's no place I'd rather be. My hard-on wages a battle to escape from my jeans. I want her more than I've ever wanted any woman.

Her hips grind against my face, her nails dig into my skull, and she rocks into my mouth, driven by a need I'm sure only I can quench. I lick faster, kiss her more greedily, flick my tongue against her sweet clit until she's locked her legs around my head. "Oh God, don't stop, I'm coming, don't stop, I'm coming," she cries out.

I want to tell her I'd never stop, but I can barely breathe, because she's coming all over my lips, my chin, my face. She sings my name as her orgasm blasts through her until she shudders and shakes, panting "oh God" in a softer voice as she comes down from the high.

As I straighten up and wipe my hand over my mouth, I take in the sight in front of me. Natalie's on her desk, her legs wide open, her beautiful face colored with pure satisfaction, her blond hair a wild tumble.

Bliss. Fucking bliss.

She blinks open her eyes, and it's as if she's waking up after a dream. When her gaze finds mine she smiles, and it's a new one—a dopey grin that somehow turns me on even more.

Impossibly, the spark in me shoots higher when she raises her arm, reaching for me. I take her hand, tug her closer, and help her off the desk. I figure she'll smooth her skirt, fluff her hair, something like that.

Instead, she turns around, bends over, and places her palms on the desk.

An offering.

She doesn't need to ask twice. I unzip my jeans, pull down my briefs, and rub the head of my cock against all that wetness. Pride surges in me. She's soaked because of me. She's dripping because I made her come so fucking hard.

Then sanity comes to roost. "I should grab a condom," I mutter.

She shakes her head. "We're fine. As long as you haven't been with anyone since—"

"Fuck no."

"Then give me your dick, Wyatt," she says with a dirty little wink.

"Take it, sweetheart. Fucking take it," I growl, as I rub the head between her legs and shove inside.

She gasps, and just like that, I'm fully nestled in the woman who's still my wife. Though something is terribly wrong about that little situation, it feels strangely right at this moment, too. But I can't dwell on titles or labels when I've got my woman to fuck. My hands grip her hips, and I raise her ass up a bit, finding the perfect angle.

It's so fucking good as I fill her, as I pull back, as I drive deep inside. She's with me every second, and we move in a kind of fevered unison. Fast, hard strokes. Deep, powerful thrusts. Groans and grunts that layer on top of each other. I roll my hips and drive in, and she rocks with me, giving me her body for *our* pleasure.

Within minutes, she's returned to the edge. She grips the sides of the desk and calls out my name. "Oh God, Wyatt. Oh my fucking God," she screams, and the sound of my name on her lips makes my balls tighten. Pleasure climbs in me, reaching a peak as I fuck her through her second climax, her orgasm coating my dick.

As she shudders beneath me, I erupt. "Fuck, Nat. Gonna come so hard."

"Yes," she urges, and I move my hands to her shoulders, holding her in place.

"So. Hard," I groan as I thrust. My body burns white-hot, and an orgasm barrels through me, torching me with pure, carnal pleasure as I come inside her with a loud, "Fucking love it."

"Me, too. Oh God, me too."

I collapse on her, my chest on her back, crushing her. She murmurs softly, a sweet hum that tells me she likes my body on hers, so I stay. I kiss her cheek then brush a soft caress on her lips. "I've wanted to do that again ever since I woke up in Las Vegas with you."

She sounds surprised when she says, "You have?"

I nod against her. "So much. It's ridiculous how much."

"Same here. Every time you're near me, I want to touch you, kiss you, feel you again."

I smile against my better judgment. "I swear it's even better sober than drunk."

"It's intoxicating in a whole new way," she says.

"Couldn't agree more." I dust a kiss on her cheek then sigh happily. Because I am happy. I'm hopped up on endorphins right now. I run my nose through her hair. Inhaling her. I can't get enough. "How was your day?"

"It was good. It's much better now, though."

"Everything good at the office?" I ask playfully.

"Everything is great at the office, especially after hours."

I rap my knuckles against her desk. "This is a most excellent desk. Be sure to tell your boss he did a fantastic job picking it out."

She jabs her elbow back into my chest. "I picked it out."

"Hmm. Well, then," I say, dropping another kiss to her forehead. "You have excellent taste in office furniture."

But after the bedroom talk ends and we clean up, I'm not sure where we go from here. The matter is solved for me when Natalie says in her most business-like voice, "Want to go over how to get an uncontested divorce in New York?"

And man, nothing sobers you up faster than that.

CHAPTER TWENTY-THREE

A siren blares.

As the red fire truck barrels up Central Park West on Saturday morning, the tan Chihuahua I'm walking along the inside path points his snout in the air.

I lift a hand to my forehead like a batter waiting to see if the ball soars out of the ballpark. "And it's heading for the bleachers! Almost there!"

The dog's mouth is closed but his nose is poised, and anticipation winds through me with the possibility that I might win big in the dog bingo game we play. Because when a dog you're walking erupts in a howl, you get *all t*he points.

I stare at the seven-pounder trotting by my side, waiting, waiting, waiting for the hound to cry out.

Nick is next to me, his hand wrapped around the leather leash of a Jack Russell Terrier, who's making a temporary home at the Little Friends rescue where we volunteer. He smirks as his dog emits a soft whine. "Maybe you'll win, or maybe I'll school you," he says, just before his dog unleashes the most epic howl I've ever heard.

His white and brown beast proceeds to imitate a wild animal for the next thirty seconds, sounding thoroughly adorable until the fire truck's siren begins to fade in the distance.

"Man," I say, dejected, as the dogs resume their usual sniff-and-trot pace. "I'm having the worst luck this week."

First, there was the knee whack, then my dumbass disposal of a delicious sandwich, and on top of that is my zombie of a marriage. I just can't kill the undead union with ordinary weapons. I'm going to have to go *The Walking Dead* style and take it down at the brain stem with a full-scale divorce attack.

It's like a hangover that won't quit.

But the really bad luck is Natalie's 180-degree turn after our glorious office sexcapades. No more workplace vixen. Instead, she's Miss Prim and Proper, zoned in on the most mind-numbing, soul-stealing thing ever . . . paperwork.

"Rough week?" Nick asks, clapping me on the back. "Did you get friend-zoned by a hooker again?"

"Yeah. The one I'm taking to your wedding," I say, giving it right back at him.

"Ouch." As we near Little Friends, Nick clears his throat. "Speaking of my nuptials . . ."

"Let me guess. You want me to become an officiant so I can pronounce you man and wife."

"Wow, no," he says, shaking his head adamantly. "Like, never ever."

"Your loss. I'd be good with that," I say, then my mind races back to Vegas, grabbing at bits and pieces of my wedding with no real luck. It's still just Elvis, sideburns, and *I do*.

"I was actually hoping you'd be my best man."

I stop in my tracks, strangely surprised that Nick asked me. "I thought you'd want Spencer to be your best man."

My twin brother shrugs. "Yeah, but you're stuck sharing DNA with me, so there's that."

I wipe a nonexistent tear from my eye. "Wow, that was heartfelt. So touching."

"Seriously, though. I mean it, Wyatt. No joking now. You helped me realize how much Harper meant to me. You gave it to me straight and helped me see that my feelings for her were real. Hell, you're my brother no matter what. But you also gave me a kick in the ass when I needed one."

I lift my foot and pretend to whack his butt outside Central Park. "I'm excellent at administering ass-kickings."

"I have no idea how this happened, but you give weirdly good advice when it comes to women. And I want you to be the one standing with me when we tie the knot."

I clap him on the back. "Hey, giving advice about you and Harper was easy. You guys are two peas in a pod. You're like gibbons."

He arches an eyebrow in question.

"Did you know that along with termites, bald eagles, swans, and beavers, they're one of the rare pairs of animals that mate for life?"

"I did not know that about gibbons. But now my brain has been expanded."

"I could tell as soon as I saw the way you looked at her that she was your gibbon," I say, and hold up a fist for knocking. "Better than a termite."

He laughs. "Harper is definitely my gibbon. And way cooler than a termite."

"Also, let me just add that I look really fucking good in a tux." I make like I'm adjusting a bowtie as we wait at the crosswalk.

Nick gestures from him to me and back. "We're both handsome devils, even if I'm handsomer."

"Hey, King of Words, you do know that handsomer is not a word people use?"

"But they should, when it comes to you and me," he says, and as we cross the street, I reflect on Nick's comment about good advice. I can recall precisely what I said to him about Harper—how he needed to man up and face his feelings for her. The question dangles before me—since I gave my brother that sage advice, what would I tell myself? How would I advise *me* to handle my situation with Natalie? But I draw a blank.

"It'd be an honor to be your best man," I tell Nick, since at least I have an answer to his request. "Especially since you're definitely stuck with me. I'm like a dog howl. I'm contagious." That gives me an idea. "Hey, what if *I* howled? Are there points for that?" I raise my chin to the skies and do my best wolf call.

And my Chihuahua goes ape-shit.

"Better late than never," I say to the pooch.

At Little Friends, we return the dogs to the rescue manager, a cute brunette named Penny. Her hair is swept up in a high ponytail, and she has a tattoo of some kind of flower on the top of her shoulder blade, one I haven't seen on her before.

"Nice ink," I say when she turns around.

Absently, she runs her hand along her neck and flashes a bright smile. "Thanks, just had it done. And how are my favorite guys?"

"Oh, we're grand," Nick says, drumming his hand on the counter.

Penny laughs and shakes her head. "I meant Turbo and Charger," she says, pointing to the dogs we walked, who are now romping in an open play area behind her. Gotta love a shelter that gives badass names to little dudes.

"Those guys are rad. They totally live up to their names," I say.

"Good to hear. Someone is coming in later to check out Charger," she says, gesturing to the dog Nick walked. She crosses her index and middle finger. "I'm hoping it works out. The guy who's coming in just wanted to make sure he's not a big barker or howler. Apartment concerns and all. Was he noisy when you walked him? Because he's good here."

My spine straightens, and Nick gulps then quickly weighs in. "He only howls at fire trucks."

Penny's nose crinkles. A small constellation of freckles is splashed across it. "Maybe Turbo is best for him, then."

I shrug happily and nod. "Yeah, and that little Chihuahua is one cool canine, so let's hope it works out."

She holds up her palm and high fives me then Nick. "Thanks again, guys. See you on Friday?"

"We'll be here," I say, then point to her iPhone. It's plugged into a base behind her, and is playing a cool tune. "Love that band. Heard them for the first time the other week."

"Me, too," she says, her hazel eyes blazing with excitement. "I love finding new music."

Nick clears his throat and jumps in, "Hey Penny, did you know Wyatt can howl?"

Penny raises an eyebrow. "You don't say?"

"He's a man of many talents. He can build you a house, he can cook a killer omelet, he can track down awesome new tunes, and he can bark at the moon. He's also free on Friday night if you—"

And my hand darts out to cover Nick's mouth. "I *was* free on Friday. But I just booked a job for Friday night."

Penny laughs at our antics. "Thanks for walking the dogs, guys."

When we leave, Nick tips his forehead toward the rescue. "What's the deal? You've been hot for Penny for months. And you don't ask her out? I was fluffing her for you."

I shrug. "Just got stuff going on."

"You mean you turned celibate?"

I snort. "Not celibate. I assure you."

Nick stares at me for several long seconds. He squints as if he's thinking hard about something, then raises an eyebrow. "Did something happen in Vegas?"

I stop short on the sidewalk. "What does that have to do with anything?"

"You've been acting different since then."

"No idea what you're talking about," I say, even though inside I'm wondering how the hell my brother became so fucking observant.

"Seems a few months ago you'd have happily jumped at the chance to chat up Penny. She's perfect for you. So all I can figure is something went down in Vegas with Natalie, and that's why you're not pursuing things with Penny." Nick gets in my face and stares at me with big bug eyes. "Who's giving good advice now?"

I shove his chest lightly. "What was the advice in that? Sounded more like an observation, and not even an accurate one." It's not that I don't trust my brother and not that I don't want to get into it with him.

The big issue is I haven't got a clue what to do about Natalie, and I'm not ready to start blabbing about our little fucked-up union to everyone. That's not fair to her. "And on that note, I've got somewhere to be."

I'm meeting Natalie soon.

As I catch the subway to head downtown, I half wish I had asked out Penny. Mostly, though, I wish I wanted to. I wish I wanted to ask anyone else on a date half as much as I want to grab a coffee with a woman who's on her way to becoming my ex-wife.

CHAPTER TWENTY-FOUR

Before I see Natalie, I make a planned pit stop in Greenwich Village to see Chase.

I hold the yellow and black magnetic tool up to the wall in the apartment, scanning the plaster surface. "The problem is, this stud finder pretty much goes off constantly when I'm around," I deadpan.

"Har, har, har," Chase says as I search for the studs in the living room wall of the one-bedroom he's considering leasing. "Think you'll ever retire that joke?"

I shake my head as I rap my knuckles against the wall. "Some jokes never get old. Anyway, here are the studs, so we can set up shelves no problem. I know you want lots of them to show off to the ladies all the big books you've read. But you probably won't even get any chickadees back to your pad, on account of you being so ugly."

He sighs deeply. "You're right. I won't get them here. Because they won't be able to wait to climb me like a tree. They'll be all over me in the elevator."

I drop the stud finder into my back pocket then make a persistent beeping noise. "Oh man, it won't stop going off with me right here."

"It's finding me, obviously," he says, leaning against the doorframe of his potential living room.

I point a finger at him. "See? Even you can't resist. You cannot deny the power of the stud finder joke."

He swings his gaze around the empty apartment. The leasing agent let him take a final look before he signs. He asked me to join him to make sure the place didn't have any hidden structural issues. Not that he'd be on the hook for them, but we've both heard horror stories of renters moving into crumbling apartments and then battling landlords for repairs. Best to make sure the home is in solid shape beforehand, and this one looks good. That's all the more remarkable since it's an older building, and it's on a great block with a cobbled sidewalk and cool restaurants.

Chase gestures to the naked floors and walls. "This place is a steal, huh?"

"Yeah, snap it up for sure."

"Awesome. I think I'll just go see the leasing agent now. When I asked her for the keys to check it out, all I had to do was flash my killer smile and she handed them over. She's hot for me." He bats his hazel eyes as he grins. "She gave me a discount on account of me being so handsome."

I roll my eyes. "Dude, she did not give you a discount. One, you're not Henry Cavill, or the shortstop for the New York Yankees. You don't have that sort of pull. Second, it's New York. No one gets a break on an apartment."

"You're just jealous of my amazing ability to land the ladies like that." He snaps his fingers. Then, in an instant, his tone downshifts to serious. "So, what's the deal with your wife?"

I lean against the kitchen doorway and sigh heavily. We both let go of the jokes. "Shit, man, I don't know. I can't figure out what the hell to do." I tell him the latest so he knows the score—our annulment went AWOL, we fucked like bunnies on her desk, and afterward she became the Queen of Do-It-Yourself-Divorce.

With a frown, Chase scratches his head. "You got me. I'm stumped."

"C'mon, Doctor Brain. You're never stumped."

"No, I mean I don't get what the problem is." He slams a fist against the other palm. "You could just bang her."

I cringe. "That's a little crass. Besides, it's not like that."

"No. It *is* like that."

I shake my head. "It's hard to separate all the stuff."

"You mean you've never had sex without feelings?"

"Of course I have. I meant it's hard to separate all the other . . . entanglements. Like the fact that I'm her employer."

He taps the right side of his skull. "You put the sex in the sex portion of your head." He raps the left side. "You put the work in the work portion." He wipes one palm against the other. "Done."

I shake my head, amused. "And my sister wonders why I call you a dog."

His eyes light up, and his expression shifts from jaded playboy to eager beaver. "Your sister asks about me?"

I roll my eyes. "Don't get any ideas. Besides, after what you just said about different portions of your brain, you can stay the fuck away from my sister."

"I'm just giving you a hard time. About all of this, including the banging." Now he's got his bedside manner in
full swing. No teasing, no fucking around. "You know
what you need to do. You care about this woman, like I
said before. When that happens, there are no separate
parts, so you've got to shut it down." He slices his hands
through the air. "She's your employee, so you just can't go
there."

That's what I love about Chase. Half the shit he says is
to get a rise out of me, and I respect the hell out of that
kind of commitment to ribbing. But when it comes right
down to it, the man gets that there are rules of the road,
and I need to follow them.

"You're right. I've got to keep the dick in the box."

He mimes opening a gift box at his waist, and I nod in
agreement then point to the hardwood floors. "And you
and your different brain parts should definitely get this
apartment. It's a good deal."

"I think I will. Thanks for checking it out. And hey, if
you want a little practice session on how to behave around
Natalie, you both should come over to Max's next
weekend. He wanted to throw me a little welcome-back-
to-town dinner-thing," Chase says, mentioning his brother.

"I'm in. And I'll ask Natalie, too."

He smacks his forehead. "Oh. Forgot to tell you. She'll
be there. Josie is planning it with Max, so she invited Natalie."

I roll my eyes. "You're always up to something."

"That pretty much describes me perfectly. Oh, and
good luck with that little problem of not being able to separate sex and feelings," he says with an arched eyebrow as
we leave.

"You got a pill for that, too, Doctor Dick?"

He gestures to his crotch. "Yeah it's called Stud Finder." He thrusts his pelvis once. "And it all points *here* for the ladies."

The thing is Chase is all talk. He was madly in love with some girl during his residency, and, well, let's just say it didn't work out the way he wanted it to.

He's right, though. There's more at stake with Natalie than my white-hot desire to bang her brains out night and day. Or my wish to take her to Coney Island and ride the rollercoaster, or take her to a barbecue, or have her be the one by my side at Nick's wedding.

What's at stake is *her*.

Natalie has a job that matters to her. The more we mess around, the more I risk putting her in an awkward employment situation. Obviously, I'd never fire her because of this, but I want her to feel comfortable at work. I've got to respect the woman's ability to pay her own bills, and since I'm the one who signs her checks, I can't let my dick, loyal prick that he is, call the shots.

That's not the kind of man I want to be.

If I keep screwing her, where does that leave her when it all goes south? And it will go south. It's inevitable. Relationships always do, especially when they start at the office.

CHAPTER TWENTY-FIVE

Natalie waits for me at a coffee stand in the Union Square Farmer's Market, with a bag of strawberries in one hand and a drink in the other. She waves hello, then gives me the beverage. "The way you like it," she says, and her comment tugs at something in my chest.

Knowing someone's coffee order isn't a big deal in the grand scheme of life, but making the effort to get the cup of joe just right is one of those little things that can make you smile.

However, smiling feels terribly out of place right now. We grab one of the little green tables set up by the edge of the market, surrounded by hipsters chowing down on falafels and drinking ginger sodas. I spin a chair around and park myself in it, resting my forearms over the back. I down a gulp of the coffee and thank her again.

Natalie tucks a strand of her blond hair behind her ear and flashes a quick grin as she sets the strawberries on the table. Dipping her hand into her purse, she grabs some papers. "I downloaded the packet yesterday for an uncontested divorce in New York. There are a ton of forms, and most don't really apply, but we should go through them anyway. As I understand it, the whole process could take anywhere from six weeks to a few months."

"Whoa. Why so long?"

"New York makes you jump through hoops."

She shuffles through forms about division of marital property, liability for joint debts, child custody and support, spousal maintenance, insurance benefits, and a ton of other legal details that make my head spin *Exorcist* style. Oh, yeah—they also remind me I'm a complete douche for suggesting we get married that night. What was supposed to be fun and daring has turned into a helluva knot to untangle.

I shake my head. "Damn, this really makes me feel like a world-class idiot for proposing in the first place. I had no clue it would turn into such a clusterfuck," I say through a heavy sigh.

"Me, neither. But what can you do but roll up your sleeves?" She slaps on a smile, and I've got to say, I'm impressed she's rolling with the mess we made of being adults. Then she whispers conspiratorially, "It's like we're the naughty kids who snuck out late with the car. But rather than enjoy the thrill of a midnight joyride, we plowed down our neighbor's mailbox, and now we're doing extra chores to pay for it."

I crack up. "Why do I have the feeling you're speaking from experience?"

She points a thumb at herself. "This girl did that."

"No shit?"

"Sixteen and far too dangerous for her own good."

"Since we're playing confessional," I open with a drawl, "you're looking in the mirror."

Her jaw drops. "You, too?"

"We went to my uncle's house during the summer, and I took out his Cadillac and accidentally drove over his neighbor's rose bushes. He was not happy. I had to catch a train to Jersey every Saturday that summer to mow his lawn and trim the hedges to make up for the cost of the roses."

She holds up a hand and we smack palms. "Does this make us the black sheep of our families?"

"Baa . . ." I say, imitating that animal.

Her eyes light up. "Can you make animal noises?"

"You want more?"

She nods excitedly. "Horse, please."

I shake my head quickly and make a neighing sound.

Holding up a finger, she asks for one more. I decide to break out my seal bark, with a throaty *arf, arf, arf* that cracks her up.

"Encore, encore!"

I shake my head. "That's all you get from Wyatt's World of Animal Sounds for now. If you're a good girl, I'll show you the lion in my repertoire later."

"I can't wait."

I rub my palms together. "Back to Adult Land."

We return to the papers, reviewing them. The one that catches my attention like a house on fire is division of marital property. Narrowing my eyes, I stab the pages with my finger. "What's this? Is that like my apartment or the business or something?"

She pats my hand gently. "Don't worry. I'm not going to make a claim on your business."

I straighten. "Didn't think you were," I say in a testy tone and grab the coffee, but apparently bringing the cup to my lips is too daunting a process, and I succeed in spilling some on my jeans. "Fuck," I curse, and Natalie grabs some napkins from her purse and hands them to me.

"Everything okay?" she asks as I wipe at the denim.

"Yeah." I meet her eyes. "My ex from long ago tried to dig into my business. Seeing that paper just kind of . . ."

"Touched a nerve?" she supplies softly.

I nod. "Stupid, I know."

"It's not stupid. It's how you feel. I'd probably be the same."

I drag a hand through my hair. "You're not like that. I shouldn't even be thinking it."

She rubs my arm. "You're right. I'm not like that. But I get it. I swear I do."

"You do?"

"It makes sense that you'd feel that way. And look, I'd be a little freaked, too, if I were you. You built a successful business. But you have my word, Wyatt. I'm not trying to get a piece of it. We didn't have a real marriage. We just had a ridiculously fun one that was only ever supposed to last for twenty-four hours. I want this process to go as smoothly as possible, too."

"Thanks for understanding. It was just one of those things I never saw coming," I say, then share a few more details of Roxy.

"That's crazy," she says, shaking her head. "No wonder—"

I tilt my head when she breaks off. "No wonder what?"

She waves a hand in front of the pages. "No wonder it would touch a nerve, that's all. If you want to get a lawyer to handle this, I understand."

I scoff and hold up my hands. "No. I swear I don't. I had more than enough of lawyers with Roxy's antics. Same with someone who hacked my site several months ago. Had to get an attorney involved then, too. I don't get why it's so hard just to stick to the plan. Pretty sure the contract for the website didn't call for her to hack into it at a later date," I say, sarcastically. "I just want to put this all behind us."

She flashes a too-bright smile. "Agreed. No sharks needed. Let's keep moving forward."

We spend the next twenty minutes reviewing paperwork and signing documents. When we're done and she puts the pages away, I lift my cup. "Tell me something fun. Something to get the taste of divorce out of my mouth."

She grabs a strawberry, twists off the leafy top, and pops it between her lips. "Strawberries taste good. But they're not actually berries. Did you know that?"

"I did not. But I like where this is going. Do continue."

"Thought you might like that little nugget, since you're a collector of quirky facts."

"What are they, if not berries? Just a regular fruit?"

She shakes her head and pops another one past her pretty red lips. After she eats, she answers, "A fleshy receptacle for seeds."

I crinkle my nose. "That's kind of gross. Where'd you learn that?"

"I looked it up the other day. I guess quirky facts were on my mind because of you." She hands me a red berry. As I eat it, I can't help but grin at something as simple as her researching life's oddities for that reason. "Your turn," she says. "Tell me something from Wyatt's Encyclopedia of Quirky Animal Facts."

"Do you know why cats can slide under a vanity cabinet in the bathroom like they're boneless?" I begin, and there's nothing quite like the old cats-have-no-collarbones factoid to take the sting out of divorcing the woman you fucked on her desk last week. In fact, collarboneless cats are pure gold when you need a conversational lubricant. I also work in a little tidbit about domesticated turkeys (they can't fly), facts about elephants (with forty thousand muscles in their trunks, they can use them to pick up tiny objects including a small coin), and a bit of insight into fish (they drink water through osmosis rather than their mouths).

Natalie smiles and laughs through my *lesson,* as she calls it. "Your fascination with animal facts—where did that come from?"

"I used to read *National Geographic* as a kid. Which probably sounds weird, since everyone thinks Nick and Josie are the smart ones."

She shoots me a quizzical look. "Who thinks that?"

I shrug. "Dunno. But probably everyone, I figure, since they *are* the smarter ones. Josie is great with books, and Nick is just . . . well, he's Nick. The old noggin works really well on him. They did better in school than I did."

"You already know where I stand on that front," she says, and holds up a fist. "Black sheep united."

I knock her curved fingers. "Seems we've got some things in common, the-almost-former-Mrs. Hammer."

"Such a shame, since it's a fun last name."

"It is. By the way, I'm assuming the fact that we're meeting at the farmer's market, not the office, means we're trying not to fuck like bunnies again?" I ask, aiming to make light of the situation.

She cracks up and gestures to the tents peddling asparagus, arugula, and artichokes. "What? You think I won't tug you behind one of the veggie stands so we can get it on behind a box of portobellos?"

Immediately, I scan the market. "Where are those damn mushrooms?"

She swats me, and we make our way out of the market. "I do think we should try to be good boys and girls," she says, her tone a touch more serious. "That work for you?"

I drape an arm over her shoulder. "Works for me. And it looks like we survived keeping our hands off each other, thanks to your mushroom strategy. Don't think it's gone unnoticed that there are no mushroom stands here today."

She snaps her fingers in an "aw shucks" gesture. "You figured me out." Her eyes drift to my hand on her shoulder, as if to say she's caught me.

I hold out that hand, admitting my guilt. "I'm trying, woman. I'm trying to be a good guy."

And I am. I'm trying so fucking hard not to hike her over my shoulder, carry her through the crowds, and kiss the hell out of her on top of the crates of berries, boxes of asparagus, or behind the bunches of bananas.

Because really, getting it on with her at a banana stand would absolutely be our style.

"Check out that banana stand," I say with a tip of my forehead and a wiggle of my eyebrows.

She swats me. "You're bad. We're trying to be friends."

I straighten and adopt a serious tone. "I meant as friends, of course. I want to be friendly with you behind the banana stand."

She rolls her eyes. "Speaking of being friends, I'll send you those videos later. I'm ready to show them to you."

When I click on the email that evening, I vow to focus on helping her, not nailing her.

Because she needs the help.

These videos suck.

CHAPTER TWENTY-SIX

When Natalie dropkicks the wiry dude in the black sweats, he falls to the floor in a graceful heap.

As if he's practiced the move before.

"See?" I say, pointing at the video playing on her phone on Monday night at the dojo, McKeon Karate. "It's like he's done it before. It reads like an ad rather than a real-life situation."

We sit cross-legged on the blue mats. She finished her classes for the night and asked me to meet her here to review the videos, since I worked late at Violet's on the kitchen remodel. This is the only chance we've had all day to connect.

She tightens her ponytail, tugging on the strands. Wearing her karate uniform, she looks tough and no-nonsense in the white pants and matching shirt, as well as the black belt. Her feet, though, are adorably cute. They're bare, and her toenails are painted in alternating shades of mint green and bright purple. Just like she told me in Vegas she liked to do.

"It's too slick, you mean?" she asks.

I tap my nose. "Bingo."

"You think it needs to feel more authentic?"

"You're trying to reach a broader audience with these videos. Inspire women to learn self-defense. You want the videos to feel more natural, in my opinion. Like this *could* happen and you'd be able to whip around and knock some fucking bastard to his knees."

She stretches forward and flops her face down on the mat. "Thank God," she says in a long exhale. "I thought you were going to say they were dull."

"Ha. No," I say, brandishing the phone. "This guy is just so *Karate Kid*. I watch this and I don't think *self-defense*. I think two karate experts doing something I can never do. It's very . . . choreographed."

She sits up straight, turns to face me, and grabs my arm. "I can do this, Wyatt. I can fix them. I've shown them to people here, and they all say they're great, but I knew deep down they weren't." She pokes my shoulder. "Thank you for being honest with me. I needed someone outside of the world of martial arts."

I officially decide Natalie is one of the coolest people I know. I've never seen someone take criticism as well as she does. She's not defensive; she's not annoyed. She truly wants to make her videos the best they can be.

Also, look at us rocking it in the friendship department.

Note to self: Focusing on helping your employee pursue her passion is a much more noble use of your time than planning how to screw her senseless again.

Yup. This is how I can be a good guy. This is Wyatt post-greasy salad.

She stands and paces around the studio. It's only us now. She's locked up for the night. "Okay, so we want this to feel real. Like some guy just came up to me on the street."

"Absolutely."

"I'm walking along, he tries to grab me . . ." She reaches for my arm and tugs me up from the floor. "Do it."

I blink. "What?"

"Attack me."

"Are you crazy?"

"No." Her blue eyes are wild. "I have an idea." She runs over to her phone, sets it up on a wooden chair at the edge of the mat, and taps the screen. "Let's do this."

"Wait," I say, when it fully hits me what her plan is. I point at my chest. "*I'm* doing this with you?"

"The videos were too slick. You've never done karate before, right?"

"Right."

"And you want to help me?"

"I do."

"Let's make it authentic," she says, then moves in closer to me and parks her hands on my shoulders. "Be my guinea pig."

And there's no way I can say no to her. No way at all, and my yes has nothing to do with wanting her underneath me and everything to do with wanting to help her chase her dreams. "Okay, ninja girl. Make me your crash-test dummy."

She takes my arm, turns away from me, and wraps it around her throat. "You're about to choke me."

"Nat, I'm not into that kind of play," I chide.

Over her shoulder, she narrows her eyes, and they are a steely blue now. "Just do it, Hammer."

I tighten my grip, and then in a split second, the breath is knocked out of me as she jabs an elbow in my stomach and throws me to the ground.

"Oomph."

Splayed on the floor of the karate studio, I stare up at Natalie like a dazed cartoon character. Her bare foot is parked on my belly triumphantly, a military leader conquering the enemy.

"Well, yeah. Like that," I say dryly.

"Should we see how that looked?"

She grabs the phone, kneels next to me, and plays the video. And hot damn. The woman is a beast. "You are fucking impressive."

"We're a good team," she says, nudging me playfully. "You don't know these moves, which makes it feel more natural. Like this is what could really happen if I were defending myself. I won't full-on attack you, but I'll do the moves and just hold back a little. Will you do more with me?"

"Do they all have to be surprise attacks?"

She pouts. "Did it hurt?"

I try to be tough. "Not really."

"Then I have faith you can handle it." She pops up, and I follow her, unsure what the next move is. But that's the point. "Let's do it. Let's make it as real as it can be."

I shrug happily. "Promise me one thing."

She flinches momentarily when I say *promise me*, but then simply nods. "What is it?"

I cup my dick. "Don't kick me in the balls."

With a quick move, she reaches for the jewels but doesn't quite touch—just darts her hand near enough to tempt me. An inch away, maybe. She brings her face close to mine and whispers sexily, "I promise I won't hurt your beautiful balls."

A bolt of lust charges through me. And while I'm glad she won't hurt 'em, I can't deny I'd really like her to play with them . . . *right about now.* Dip her hand into my jeans, down inside my boxer briefs, and right the fuck over the goods. I nearly groan as my imagination cuts loose on such a simple but smoking-hot image. She's fired up for karate, though, so I call cut on the porn reel the movie camera in my mind wants to shoot.

Bouncing on her toes, Natalie tells me how to go after her next. She walks across the mat, her back to me, and I sneak up from behind and try to drag her away.

She's fast and furious, moving in a blur as she kicks me and sends me crumpling to the ground. I'm down on my hands and knees. I'm not wounded; I'm just winded because I'm surprised. She came at me so fast, like a sandstorm.

"Wouldn't want to meet you in a parking garage." I catch my breath.

When I raise my face, she beams at me. "Ready for more?"

"Hit me with your best shot, Frisky Mittens."

And so she does. She gives me a simple direction then takes me down. Then she does it again in a whole new way. After twenty minutes of abuse, I'm lying on the blue mat, spent from that hell of a workout. She could take me in any battle. "You win," I say, breathing hard.

"That was amazing." After she switches off the camera, she flops down next to me and turns on her side. "But seriously. Are you okay?" She runs her hand along my arm.

I shudder from her touch, but do my best to hide the reaction. "*Now* the woman asks if I'm okay," I say to the ceiling.

"But you are, right?"

I laugh and turn to look at her. "I swear, I'm fine."

She grabs my arm in excitement. "You're the best. You helped me so much. It means so much to me that you did this. You didn't have to, but you did it anyway."

Mission accomplished. I give myself a mental pat on the back for my laser focus on building her up, not screwing her sideways. "I'm glad I could do it. I might also be a glutton for punishment."

"Be *my* glutton," she says. Her face glows, and she looks healthy, radiant, energized. She's totally in her element. It's also incredibly hot, which is exceedingly dangerous.

So I say nothing.

Silence descends on us, the kind of quiet that's rich with possibilities. Somehow, saying nothing seems to suggest something else—the other things we could do right about now. Her smile fades, but it's not replaced with sadness. Instead, she studies me intently, and I do the same with her. Taking in the way her hair falls from the ponytail holder. Registering how her chest rises with each breath. Noticing how her blue eyes are darker when she looks at me this way.

It's a look I recognize. One I want desperately. It's how she looks before she kisses me. She nibbles on the corner of her lips and tiptoes her fingers up my shoulder, then snatches them away. "Sorry. I'm trying to be good."

"Me, too," I say, my voice dry.

Hers is a soft whisper. "It's hard."

I sigh. "So hard sometimes."

"Is it working? Being good?"

"I want to be a good guy, Natalie."

"You are a good guy, Wyatt. You're here."

I park my hands under my head, as if I'm cuffing them. "And that proves I'm succeeding?

She nods. "I think so."

"You give me more credit than I deserve," I say, and let my gaze drift to the ceiling. If I look at her, I'll try to touch her. If I stare into those eyes another second, I'll be lost in all this desire.

"You deserve more credit than you give yourself." Her tone is earnest and firm, and it hooks into me.

"I wouldn't be so sure I deserve any credit. You have no idea . . ."

She pushes up higher on her elbow. I can see her face now as she speaks. "No idea what? What it's like to work beside someone you want? What it's like to be inches away from him or her? What it's like to have that person and then fight like hell to resist that person?"

CHAPTER TWENTY-SEVEN

Dragging a hand through my hair, I try to draw a breath full of sanity, but the only thing I'm inhaling right now is the scent of her. Of how much I want her.

"I have all those ideas, too," I say harshly. "Because I'm so fucking turned on being near you. Then you say all that, and what am I supposed to do but want you even more?"

A tiny grin appears on her face. "So we're even, then."

I laugh lightly. "Even Steven."

She wiggles her eyebrows. "Look on the bright side. I told you I wouldn't hurt your beautiful balls."

"The balls and I thank you."

She licks her lips, and her next words come out like a sultry song. "How can I thank you for tonight?" Her eyes drift down my face, then she's eying my chest, my waist, and finally the bulge in my jeans that she caused.

I'm losing this battle—losing it hard. All my plans to be a good guy are shot to hell when her hand follows her eyes. "They're definitely okay?" she asks, all innocent and concerned, her palm hovering millimeters away from the package.

I shrug lightly and throw in the towel. "Can't hurt to check."

She cups me through my jeans, her palm wrapping around my cock then sliding between my legs, over the fabric of my jeans.

I hiss.

In a flurry, she straddles me, grabs my wrists, and pins them behind my head as she rocks up and down on my hard cock.

"Nat," I groan, like a warning. "What are we doing?"

She shakes her head. "I don't know. But when I get near you like this, my body takes over. I just want to touch you everywhere." She runs her nails down my chest. "Grind against your dick," she says, and demonstrates how she likes that, too.

I groan loudly. "You kill me when you say that stuff. Your dirty mouth is my guilty pleasure."

"Never feel guilty about pleasure." She lowers her face, the soft hair in her ponytail swishing against my neck and her mouth near my ear. "There's something I haven't done with you."

My muscles tighten with anticipation. "What is it?"

"I want to know what you taste like. Do you want that?"

In a second, I break free from her grip on my wrists to grab her hips, making her ride me. "So fucking much."

"You sure?"

I'm not above begging. "Please suck my dick."

Her eyes widen with desire as she rubs against me. Teasing. Deliberately toying with me.

I grasp her face and start to push her head down. "I need your mouth on me, sweetheart."

"It turns me on to hear you beg for it," she says in a sexy purr. "Can you say *please* again?"

I rock up into her, letting her feel the steel in my jeans. "Nat," I growl. "I'm begging you. Please suck me off."

She closes her eyes, the expression on her face as if she's dirty dreaming. "I want to taste you coming in my throat."

A tremor of lust rattles through my body. I've got to have her now. I push her off my crotch and point to my hard-on. "Unzip my pants and get those sexy lips wrapped around my dick. Stop talking and start sucking."

She arches an eyebrow and works open my zipper. I help her along, lifting my ass, and pushing down my jeans and briefs to my thighs. In a second, her head is between my legs, and the tease continues. It's the most fantastic kind of torture from her tongue as she flicks it over the head, leaving me wanting so much more.

"C'mon, Nat."

"C'mon what?" She lifts her face and wiggles an eyebrow. "I want to play."

"Then kiss the tip," I command and grasp the back of her head, tugging her down.

She moans as she draws the head of my cock between her warm lips. I want to sing from the pleasure. From the sheer, sweet heat of her wet tongue on my dick.

"So good," I say roughly, rubbing my dick against her lips. She moves with me, circling her tongue over the tip as I glide it across her lips. Desire rushes in my veins as I feel her hot breath on my cock.

"Lick the shaft now," I tell her, and her eyes dance naughtily as she runs her tongue from the head all the way down to the base.

I moan louder when she looks up at me as she dips her hand between my legs. Cupping my balls, she plays, dragging her nails over them. With her eyes on me, she whispers, "Want me to lick them?"

"Fuck yeah," I grunt, thrusting into her hand, urging her closer.

She bends down, brushing her tongue over me, then under, licking my balls, swirling her tongue all over them, drawing them into her mouth. Driving me motherfucking crazy. I clasp her head harder. "So fucking good," I moan.

She lets go and crawls up me, that flirty, dirty look in her eyes. "Then tell me how much you want all of my mouth."

I run my index finger over her naughty lips. "I want to fuck your pretty little mouth so bad."

Pleasure shoots through me as she inches down my body, pushing up my shirt so she can kiss my chest, my abs, my waist, then the happy trail, until she's eye to one-eye with my cock again, where I want her. "Jesus, Nat. You look so good next to my dick."

"I do believe your cock and my mouth will get along just fine," she says with a wink, then she opens wide and draws me all the way in. Holy shit. I've never been blown like this before. She's fierce, and frenzied, and just a hungry, delicious thing, sucking my dick with the most astonishing friction I've ever felt. She's fast, determined, and has a magnificent gag reflex because she takes all of me, and that's not easy.

Her lips are wrapped nice and snug around my aching erection. With each swipe of her tongue, each move of her lips, my hips shoot higher, and all I care about is coming and coming hard. She's got me on the fast track, and considering how goddamn worked up I am for her, it won't take me long.

Not with my gorgeous Natalie in control, her wicked mouth sucking my shaft and her talented fingers playing with my balls. She sends me into sensory overload, touching and playing and licking and sucking until everything below the belt lives in the land of intoxicating white-hot pleasure.

My dick whistles a happy tune, and my balls skip with joy at getting this kind of attention. Threading my hands tighter in her hair, I fuck and fuck and fuck, thrusting hard into her mouth. She gulps and sucks loudly, but doesn't let up. She takes my dick as deep as she can go, and sorry if that makes me a crass motherfucker, but there is just something about a woman this hell-bent on giving the blow job of my dreams that makes me want her even more.

And I do. I crave everything about her.

I want to wake up to this. Find her in the shower, hands on the wall, ready for me. I want to get on my knees for her and go to town on my woman. Feel her dripping all over my face as I eat her, and holy fuck . . . an orgasm charges through me as I imagine getting her off.

"Gonna come so hard."

And then I'm shooting jets into her mouth, and she sucks it down. I pant, and moan, and writhe, and don't think I'll ever be sane again.

But then suddenly I am of sound mind and body, because I know, with perfect clarity, what needs to happen next. "Get on my face, pretty girl," I say. In seconds, she's shoved off her karate pants and undies, and she straddles me, lowering herself to my mouth.

This.

Her pleasure. Her sweetness. Her intense arousal. With my hands gripping her hips, I move her over my mouth, my tongue, my lips, guiding her as she fucks my face. She covers me, and I swear I'm in another realm. She's paradise to me with her delicious, wonderful, fantastic pussy that tastes so fucking good parked on my face.

"Oh God, I'm gonna come on you," she cries out.

And with her orgasm alert, she's there, all wet and hot and wild. Her hands brace on the mat above my head as she rides me into her sweet abandon, fucking my face like it was put on this Earth for her pleasure.

It didn't take her long, but that was just enough rest time for round two. After she comes down from her high, I flip her over. She's the one pinned, and that's how I want her.

"Now who's flat on her back?" I wiggle an eyebrow as I grab her knees, push them up her chest, and slide into her hot, tight pussy.

"Oh fuck," she moans, arching her spine as I push deep in her, bracing on my arms, my palms by her shoulders. Like that, I take the reins. She's been the star of the show, sucking my dick and riding my face, and now I want to be the man on top. Fucking her. Taking her. Having her. Making sure she knows how much pleasure I can bring her.

As I sink into her hot center, she lifts her hips, rocking her sexy little body up against me.

"Spread your legs for me," I tell her. "Nice and wide. I want to watch as I fuck you."

With a carnal moan, she opens her thighs even wider for me. I watch where our bodies meet, just fucking stare as my dick fills her. "Look at us," I say huskily.

She follows my gaze and trembles as she stares at my cock, gliding in and out of her. "We look hot, Wyatt."

I bring my thumb to her swollen clit, rubbing it as she watches me stroke in and out of her pussy. She turns even slicker as she stares. I lower myself, my chest pressed to her beautiful body as I rub her clit. "I can't stand it," I grit out. "I can't fucking stand how much I want you."

Then she shudders and digs her nails into my ass. Her head falls back, her neck exposed, and she shatters. She falls apart beneath me, coming and crying out, and shouting, "Oh god, oh god, oh god, oh god."

An endless series of *oh gods* rips the air, and I follow her there, chasing my own release, grunting and groaning, and loving how fucking good we are together.

Then, footsteps sound in the hall, the clack of soles on the floor.

Natalie's eyes go wide, and I scramble off her, my dick still hard and covered in us. She pops up, and I've never seen someone get dressed as fast as this woman.

The click of the door unlocking lands in my ears as I yank up my briefs and jeans, then zip them closed. I don't even have time to button the top button. I just smooth a hand on my T-shirt, crumple over and moan, like Natalie landed one in my ribs.

"I didn't know you were going to do the dropkick thing in my stomach," I mutter as the door opens and a redhead with a short bob walks in.

"Oh. I didn't realize you'd still be here, Natalie. How's it going? I forgot my hairbrush."

Hairbrush? You came back for a fucking hairbrush? Learn to work the finger comb, darling.

"Hello, Mrs. McKeon. I haven't seen one," Natalie says, her tone still breathy.

Mrs. McKeon arches an eyebrow. "Looks like you could use one, though," the woman says, gesturing to Natalie's messy hair.

My heart catches with worry that she's been busted. This woman let her use the studio, and now she's going to karate chop Natalie for turning it into a bow-chicka-wow-wow pad. Natalie's cheeks imitate a beet as she runs her hand through her sex-tousled hair. "Oh, I . . ."

"She's a fierce one," I say, interjecting. "She was whooping me something good with her black belt moves."

The redhead crosses her arms. "I can't wait to see the video series when it's done, then. What moves did you work on tonight?"

"Headlocks, mostly," I say, with a straight face. "Lots and lots of headlocks."

CHAPTER TWENTY-EIGHT

Natalie: I can't keep risking my job like that. My *other* job. The karate classes.

Wyatt: I'm sorry, Nat. I feel terrible.

Natalie: Not your fault.

Wyatt: All mine. I should have been smarter. Taken you to my home or something.

Natalie: It's my fault, too. This may surprise you (not!) but I kinda love the risky sex.

Wyatt: Shocked. Shocked, I tell you.

Natalie: With you, I should add. I like it with you. It just does something to me. The danger. The chance of getting caught.

Wyatt: Um. Yeah! It's fucking hot.

Natalie: But it's so risky.

Wyatt: Definitely too dangerous . . .

Natalie: It really is. I know you tried, but when Mrs. McKeon asked me to stay after you left . . . well, let's just say, I get the impression she's not too happy with me.

Wyatt: Ah, shit. Nat. I feel terrible. What can I do to help?

Natalie: Become ugly. Act like an asshole. Stop being so damn caring.

Wyatt: Likewise, could you start acting like a cold-hearted bitch who'll stab me in the back? It'd make it so much easier to keep my hands off you.

Natalie: If you could get a reversal on your sense of humor so I wouldn't laugh so much around you, that'd also help.

Wyatt: While we're at it, please stop having so damn much in common with me.

Natalie: And another thing. Maybe you can quit trying to help me succeed at my passion.

Wyatt: And how about you cut out the crap with making me sandwiches? That was crossing a line.

Natalie: I'm glad you liked the sandwich :)

Wyatt: Um, I should confess I gave it to a homeless guy.

Natalie: That's so sweet. See? That's what I mean. You just do these things . . .

Wyatt: Wait. Before you think I'm sweet, let me be honest. I was afraid you were poisoning me.

Natalie: SO YOU TRIED TO POISON A HOMELESS PERSON INSTEAD???

Wyatt: No! I freaked out. My mind went haywire. I told you about my ex, and what she tried to do to my business. Sometimes thinking a woman is out to get me is my default setting. It was stupid and wrong to think that about you, but I did it anyway, imagining you were up to something. I tossed the sandwich, and later I found out a homeless guy had loved it, and well, I felt like a schmuck.

Natalie: That is a little schmucky.

Wyatt: A world-class schmuck, I should add. Will you forgive me?

Natalie: Yes, because you've already been punished enough by missing out on my spectacular lunch. I rock in the sandwich department.

Wyatt: Maybe I can make it up to you with a stir-fry. Or a southwestern shrimp soup. Or this new blackened catfish fajita recipe that's awesome.

Natalie: My RSVP to all three is yes. And also, I want you to know . . . I get it. I truly do. We all have fears. You have a fear of being taken. And hey, my last boyfriend was boring, so I have a fear of being bored.

Wyatt: How'd a woman like you ever wind up with a dull dude? You're the opposite. You're the most exciting, interesting, fascinating woman I've ever known.

Natalie: At the time, I thought I needed to be more serious. Less adventuresome.

Wyatt: Your sense of adventure is one of my favorite things about you, Nat.

Natalie: Ditto.

Natalie: Also, I was wrong.

Wyatt: Wrong? About what? Your sense of adventure?

Natalie: No. Remember in Vegas when I said there was no such thing as a calorie-free chocolate . . . or a guy who's funny, well hung, and sweet?

Wyatt: YOU FOUND CALORIE-FREE CHOCO-LATE?? I'm coming over.

Natalie: I wish!!! But I did come across this guy who's funny, well hung, and sweet.

Wyatt: No way. He sounds like a unicorn.

Natalie: I like unicorns.

Wyatt: I bet unicorns like you, too. I hear they like adventuresome, sexy, hot, kind, caring, organized, and totally fucking awesome babes.

Natalie: There's only one problem with this unicorn.

Wyatt: What's that?

Natalie: He's my boss.

Wyatt: Yeah, I find myself in a very similar situation with an employee.

Natalie: What are we doing, Wyatt?

Wyatt: I wish I knew, Nat. I wish I knew. All I know is I can't stop thinking about you, but I don't want to mess things up for you. At any of your jobs.

Natalie: That's the real unicorn. Having it all.

CHAPTER TWENTY-NINE

Charlotte hands me a margarita when I walk into Max's living room in his pad in Battery Park City.

"It's my secret recipe. Made with Gummi Bears," she says with a big smile.

I take the glass and down a gulp. It's cold, delicious, and mildly candy-sweet. "Not very secret since you've spilled the beans, now is it?"

She laughs and pats the cushions, so I take the seat next to her on the huge L-shaped chocolate-brown couch facing the windows. The gang's all here. Nick is parked in the corner of the sofa, with Harper curled up next to him. Chase is on the other end, and I catch a glimpse of Natalie and Josie in the kitchen with Max. Spencer is by Charlotte's side, and he raises a glass to me.

"Glad to hear you won the best-man derby. Just don't make a move on the bridesmaid," he jokes, clasping Charlotte's shoulder.

I hold up my hand. "No worries there, man. Pretty sure your wife's not the only bridesmaid who's off-limits," I say, since Harper asked Charlotte and Josie to be bridesmaids, as well as a few other friends.

"Speaking of bridesmaids," Harper says, stretching across Nick to tap my knee. "My friend Abby knows someone in need of your carpentry services. You remember her? You guys are both encyclopedias of animal facts. I'll have her reach out to Natalie."

"Excellent. Appreciate you spreading the good word for us, especially to someone who can crush it in bar trivia, too," I say, and Harper laughs. Then I lift my chin toward the view of the tip of Manhattan and mouth *nice*.

I haven't been to Max's new place, but damn, this pad is first-class. Up here on the twenty-fifth floor, there's a view of the Statue of Liberty and the Hudson River. Early evening sun shines in the floor-to-ceiling windows.

"Hey, Max," I call out, turning my head toward the kitchen. "You building cars for Seinfeld and Leno now or something? This place is out of this world."

He strides in from the kitchen with a beer in one hand and a margarita in the other, and laughs in a deep baritone. "I can't divulge all my celebrity clients."

"Oh yeah, it's privileged information," Chase says, sketching air quotes.

"How *is* business? Good, I trust?" I ask Max.

He sets down the margarita on a coaster atop a blond wood coffee table that looks to be handcrafted, and takes a swig of his beer. "You know, I really can't complain."

"I'm pretty sure that's the understatement of the year," Chase says, a note of pride in his voice. "He's killing it."

I raise my glass to Max. "To continued good fortune on the business front," I say, and gesture to the lot of us. Charlotte and Spencer's bars are bona fide hits, with three thriving locations and a fourth opening soon. Nick just launched a second late-night naughty cartoon on a premium network, and both his shows are rocking in the ratings, while Harper continues to be one of the most popular kids' magicians in New York. Josie's a star in the world of flour, and Max is the king of the custom car business in Manhattan, building beautiful, powerful vehicles from the ground up. While Chase is the golden boy, Max is the dark knight, as I like to call him. Dark hair, dark eyes, big build, and he drives a sleek car the color of midnight that would make Batman jealous.

Max taps his bottle to my glass then nods to his brother. "I'll drink to that. And to the fact that my little brother is back in town."

"Aww, you missed me," Chase says with a goofy smile.

Max smacks him on the back. "I just missed the free medical care."

"Family," Chase deadpans. "Can't live with them, can't perform a lobotomy on them without permission."

"Where's Mia?" I ask, since their sister is the only who's not here tonight.

"Mia had to go out of town on a business trip." Max points his thumb in the direction of the kitchen. "I better go check on the chicken."

I look at Chase and furrow my brow. Max is not known for his prowess at the stove. "He cooked for you?"

Chase laughs and shakes his head. "Nope. Josie and Natalie did. Did you know your wife makes the best grilled chicken?"

All conversation ceases in a heartbeat.

Spencer straightens. "What?"

My brother's jaw drops. "No fucking way."

Harper throws a pillow at me. "You didn't."

From the kitchen, Josie shrieks. "When I told you to show her the sights, I didn't mean the Little White Wedding Chapel."

My sister strides across the tiled floor, huffing and puffing, her heels clicking purposefully, and shoves me hard on the chest.

"Ouch." I crane my neck and meet Natalie's gaze from the kitchen. "Did I mention my bud has the biggest mouth in Manhattan?"

Natalie shrugs with a what-can-you-do smile. "Guess that's why cats have no collarbones. So it's easier for them to get out of the bag."

And for one brief moment, it's just me and my almost ex-wife, whose sense of humor makes me want to join her in the kitchen, kiss the hell out of her, then help her make the rest of the meal. Hell, I'd happily do dishes with her, too.

"Is this true?" Josie's green eyes are wide as she directs her question to Natalie. "And you didn't tell me?"

"Thanks, Chase, for sharing that little tidbit," I mutter at the same time.

But before Natalie can answer, Spencer's laughter booms. "Oh yes. I'll second that." He raises his margarita glass. "I can't thank you enough, Chase. You have just given me fodder for the next several years." Spencer stares at me with a cat-eating-the-canary smile. "Now, I believe we all want to hear the lovely story of how Wyatt proposed to my wife's sister."

Nick smirks at me and shakes his head. "Dude. I told you Vegas was a recipe for trouble. I knew you were up to something."

Josie whacks my elbow. "I asked you if you said something stupid to her in Vegas. I was right."

"I said 'let's get married.' Okay? There. Are you all happy?" I gesture to the crew, and all seven of them are having a big fat laugh at my expense.

"Wait." Natalie's firm voice cuts across the apartment. Everyone turns to the blue-eyed blonde in the kitchen doorway. "Why is no one getting on my case? Why is everyone on Wyatt's case? Do you think I wasn't involved? That it was just one of his big, crazy ideas? I did play a part, people. I did say yes. A lot of yeses, as a matter of fact," she says, and Josie's eyebrows shoot into her hairline at that barely veiled innuendo. "Then I said the big yes."

Harper shakes her head, her long sheet of red hair moving with her. "Is this you guys pranking us?"

"I assure you, there's no pranking." Natalie marches over to me, parks herself on my lap, holds my face, and plants a kiss on my lips. Once more, all my thoughts fade to just the two of us. Her soft lips. Her sweet breath. Her intoxicating taste. My eyes float closed, and even though this is the shortest kiss in the history of time, it still knocks the air from my lungs. When she pulls away, I feel dizzy.

Everyone else is speechless. They're just staring at us.

Natalie ends the silence. "You'll all just have to accept that Wyatt Hammer kisses me like it's the only thing he wants to do in the whole world, and I couldn't resist him. But don't worry. We're getting a divorce, and that's that. Now can we please eat?"

"Wait," Spencer says, clearing his throat. He gestures from her to me and back. "You're not together now? Because it sure seemed like you were."

Then he flinches and drops a hand to his thigh where Charlotte's squeezing his leg. "I mean," Spencer says, correcting himself, "let's eat."

When it registers what just happened—Charlotte pinched him to shut him up—I can't help but wonder what Natalie has been telling her sister.

Because Charlotte clearly knows everything I do, and maybe even more.

* * *

Josie's coconut layer cake is divine.

Chase rolls his eyes for the twentieth time. "I just want to get in a tub and bathe in this cake."

I arch an eyebrow. "A cake tub?"

Chase nods. "Absolutely. Just fill it up to the top."

Josie laughs then asks, "Should we fill it with cake batter or finished cake?"

"Finished cake. Then frosting," he answers.

She sets down her fork. "Does that mean you want to be frosted in this cake tub, too, Chase?"

He takes another bite. "With this cake, yes please." He tilts his head to the side, looking at her across the table. "By the way, I like the new 'do," he says, gesturing to her hair. Josie's a brunette, but she's dyed several strands pink.

She twirls a pink streak. "Thank you. I did it while you were gone."

"Because you missed me?"

She wriggles an eyebrow. "Ha. Yes, when I think of you, I think pink."

Soon, it's time to clear our plates, and as we clean, Natalie and I wind up alone in the kitchen at the sink. "That was . . . weird," I say.

"The way Chase flirts with your sister?"

I laugh. "Well, yeah. But the whole thing with us, too."

"Did you feel like they were staring at us all through dinner?" she asks as she rinses a dessert plate.

"Like we were in the zoo."

"I think they wanted us to kiss again."

"They weren't the only ones," I say softly, then take the plate from her hand and slide it into the dish rack.

She meets my gaze as the water runs. Her voice is soft, just for me. "They *definitely* weren't the only ones."

I run a fingertip gently along her neck, from her earlobe down to her collarbone. "Right here. I want to kiss you right here."

I demonstrate, dusting my lips ever so faintly against the delicious skin of her neck, breathing her in.

She shudders. "When you kiss me like that, it makes me forget to breathe," she whispers, then turns her face so our lips brush lightly.

And I'm the one to shudder.

When we leave, we crowd in the elevator together, Spencer with his arm around Charlotte, Nick holding hands with Harper, Chase telling Josie a story of the marble he removed yesterday from a kid's nose, and Natalie next to me. She's so close, I could hold her hand, drape an arm over her shoulder, kiss her hair.

All the things I want to do.

And I want her to go home with me tonight, too.

But she doesn't. When we reach the street, we go our separate ways.

CHAPTER THIRTY

Another conundrum confronts us several days later when Hector sleeps late again and misses work.

Natalie tries a few other guys, but they're all busy. Since I haven't expanded yet, or hired anyone regularly after the failed Vegas gig, it's all me once more, and the clock's ticking. I head uptown to Violet's home, eager to finish her remodel on time.

With a laser focus, I do nothing but work all morning. Drill hinges. Adjust doors. Hang cabinets. For her Upper East Side penthouse apartment ultra-modern kitchen redo, Violet ordered an exotic wood that looks stunning in her home and must be treated with extra care. That's precisely how I do treat it, making sure every single part lines up perfectly without a nick, scratch, or dent.

Then again, that's my job, and that's what I aim to do every time for every client.

But midway through the morning, an on-time finish appears exceedingly unlikely. There's just too much to do. I barely have time for a lunch break, but my stomach rumbles, and a bead of sweat slides down my chest from all the lifting and hammering. I need fuel in my line of work, so as I head out of Violet's building into the midday crowds and bright sun, I follow my stomach in the direction of the closest bodega. As I walk along the tree-lined, brownstone-laden block, I ring Natalie.

"Hey," I say, and I can feel a smile tugging at the corners of my mouth.

"Hey you." The sweet sound of her voice makes the grin spread all the way across my face, makes my heart flip-flop.

We're coworkers, but right now we don't sound like it. We sound like lovers. Like a boyfriend and a girlfriend. Like this is how we talk to each other when we call for no reason. And hell if I even know why I called her. Maybe just to hear her say *hey you*.

Feels like enough of a reason, and that's what I want—to be able to talk to her like this, to call her any time and chat about our days without all the other stuff hanging over us.

I drop my shades over my eyes and hoof it to the store on the corner to grab a sandwich. "How's it going at head-quarters?"

"Everything's good here in the Bat Cave," she says, then tells me what's cooking, and it's yet another day of her managing my company like a champ. This woman is invaluable to me. "And I checked in with the courts. Every-thing is on track with the divorce, too," she tells me, but I don't feel like talking about the end of our union, and it turns out I don't have to, since she segues into the next item. "I got a call today from Harper's friend Abby. The guy she works for is investing in a new restaurant, and he wants to talk to you about doing some of the cabinetry."

"Interesting," I say since I don't usually handle commercial work. But she tells me more about the job and it sounds doable. "Can you stop by after Violet's to do an estimate? I can meet you there. It's in the Village."

My chest does that wild flop again, knowing I'll see her later. Which is ridiculous, since I see her nearly every day. But I like seeing her so much. "Yeah, sounds great," I say as I turn into the bodega, grab a bag of chips and a diet soda, and get in line at the deli counter.

"So." She takes a beat. "You called. Is everything okay?"

Right. The reason for my call. What the hell was it? I stare at the glass case of the counter, hoping to find the answer in the ham. But honestly, I've never cared for ham, so that doesn't help. Then I remember why I'm on a quickie lunch break. "I don't think I can finish Violet's job today. Any chance you can track someone down for the afternoon? I just need another set of hands for a few hours."

"Why don't I come join you?"

"You sure?" I try not to sound too enthusiastic.

"We did it before at Lila's. We can do it again. I'll be there in twenty minutes."

"You're a ninja, and a goddess, and the mistress extraordinaire of the Manhattan carpentry business. Can I get you a sandwich? The turkey here looks good."

"Thanks, but I already ate. A poisoned ciabatta. I should be dead shortly."

A little later she joins me, and we set to work. Glancing over at her, carefully hammering in a nail, I'm struck once again with the realization of all she does for my business— she saves the day.

As we work, she's quiet and focused, and so am I. Around five o'clock, she takes a short bathroom break and returns quickly. I set down the tools to pour a glass of water. Natalie's working on the ladder in the kitchen, wiping the wood on a cupboard above the stove, making sure it shines. But her shoulders shake like something is terribly wrong.

"Hey, what's going on?"

"Nothing," she mutters with a gulp as she moves down a rung.

"Are you sure?"

"I'm fine."

I place a hand on her lower back. "Hey, tell me. What's wrong?"

She sucks in a deep breath and meets my gaze. Words spill from her mouth like raindrops falling. "Mrs. McKeon said she doesn't need me to teach anymore."

My jaw drops. "What?"

"She texted me earlier. I just saw her note when I was in the bathroom." Her voice catches. "She said the mats weren't in good shape after that night. I think she knows what we did there. I'm so embarrassed."

She climbs down the ladder, drops her face into her hands, and lets the tears fall. I wrap my arms around her. I don't know what to say, since it's my fault, too, so I just hold her in my arms as she cries quietly. I brush her hair away from her cheek while another tear slides down. She's a quiet crier. No sobs from her—just a steady trickle down her face. Even so, I can feel all the sadness in her, and all the shame she shouldn't have to feel.

"I don't want to be the black sheep," she whispers into my shirt.

"You're not, sweetheart," I say, gently. "I swear you're not."

"But I am. I was the wild child in high school. Maybe

then I was taking my dad's car for a late-night ride, but look at me. I'm doing it again." She pushes on my chest half-heartedly. "Taking you for a late-night ride."

I manage a small laugh at her effort to make fun of herself. "Hey. Pot, meet the kettle. Besides, neither one of your so-called sins are that bad."

"I know, but I loved that dojo. I was starting to build a reputation there."

I stroke her hair. "And your reputation will remain intact because you're amazing at what you do. We'll find another dojo. You still have your self-defense classes at the other studio, right?"

She nods against me. "It's just one class a week. The one Lila is taking."

I rest my chin on the top of her head. "That's cool that Lila's in your class."

"She's a sweet lady. Every time I see her she says she's working on getting the Vegas job restarted. She said it's looking good. But Wyatt, I just feel like a fuck-up."

I pull back from her and tuck a finger under her chin. "You're not. I'm just as guilty."

She slugs me lightly. "I should fire you, then."

"I wish I could take it for you. I would. I swear I would. I hate that this happened."

She swallows and takes a deep breath. It seems to center her. "We need to figure out what we're doing."

"I know," I say, desperation coloring my tone because I wish I had the answer to having it all. I want to keep working with her, and I want to be with her, and I want to erase our Vegas mistake and just move forward like a normal man and woman dating in Manhattan would do. But whenever we take a step, we meet a roadblock.

All I know is when she tilts her chin and looks up at me, having her in my arms feels so right. But everything goes wrong when I touch her. The botched annulment, our fight, and now her losing a karate gig.

"Wyatt," she whispers, "I want to kiss you right now, but each time I do, I feel like something foolish happens."

"Add mind-reader to your skill set, because I was thinking the same thing," I say as I gather her in my arms once more. Her back is pressed against the ladder as I leave a soft kiss on her forehead. "No making out then," I whisper, with a gentle brush of my lips on her eyelids. "Just this."

She nods against me, a soft sigh escaping her mouth. I dust my lips over her cheeks, her chin, her jaw, then hover oh so temptingly close to her lips.

"We'll be good," I tell her in the faintest voice. "For real. Let's get our divorce, and if we still feel this way, then we can figure out how the hell an ex-husband can date his ex-wife."

"Who's also his employee," she adds with a smile, and I'm putty in her hands. Because . . . that smile . . . those lips . . .

Her.

"We'll figure it all out," I say, even though the prospect of *how* feels like advanced calculus. But we'll cross that bridge when we get to it. I just hope the next few weeks till she's my ex fly by. Never would I have thought I'd want to date my ex-wife so badly. But I do. I really fucking do. Maybe that sounds crazy. Maybe it is. But I want to start over with her in a normal way. A clean slate with this woman I'm crazy for? That seems like a perfect way to begin again.

I clasp her cheeks and drop one more quick kiss on her forehead.

She parks a hand on my chest and lightly pushes. "If you keep kissing me like that, we're going to wind up doing it on this ladder, and God knows with my luck, I'll break a leg."

I stroke my chin. "The ladder, you say?"

"Don't get any funny ideas."

"Now I have one," I say, and drop to my knees and press her against the wood, my hand on her stomach. "I would love to do this to you right now." I run my hands up her legs, kissing her through the denim. "But I'm going to show you how good I can be." I wrap my hands around her ass, squeeze, and press a kiss between her legs, even though she's fully clothed. "I can be so good," I moan, as I kiss her once more through the fabric of her clothes.

She gasps, lacing her hands into my hair. I stay like that. On my knees. My lips on her jeans. Teasing her. Leaving her with very clear instructions on what I'll be doing when this moratorium ends.

"*Wyatt*," she murmurs, her grip on my hair tightening.

I push my face closer, inhaling her scent, then bite at the denim before I stand and plant a quick kiss on her forehead. "See? Wasn't I so sweet?"

Her lips curve into a grin. "You are a unicorn."

I glance down at the tent in my jeans. "I'm absolutely a unicorn right now."

She laughs then tugs me close for a tight hug. When we pull apart, we resume our work and finish the job. A little later, Violet unlocks the door, strides in, and beams. Her sleek black hair is twisted high on her head, and a slash of peach lipstick covers her mouth.

"The kitchen looks great."

"And it's done on time," Natalie declares.

Violet shakes her head in amazement. "I'm thrilled. Completely thrilled." She shifts her gaze from me to Natalie, then back. "You two are quite a team. I'm so impressed with all you've done."

When we leave to load up the tools and ladder in my truck, it occurs to me there's something terribly unjust about what just happened. Natalie was busted at the karate studio. I got off scot-free at a client's home. Fine, we weren't naked and getting it on at Violet's house, but we were intimate in a whole other way. Is what we shared on the ladder so much "safer" than what we did on the mat? Maybe. At the same time, though, I can't help but feel even closer to Natalie now, and I wish I could protect her. Keep her from getting hurt. Save her from any sort of sadness.

Regardless of what we were doing, the fact remains that she's taking the hit for what's happening between us, and I'm not. I don't know how to change the score, or if I can. All I know is I want to, and I need to figure out how.

But right now, we've got another gig, so we head to the Village to the restaurant site for the estimate. Natalie introduces me to a big strapping dude with huge arms. He's the restaurant investor, and looks like one of the Hemsworth brothers.

"Simon Travers," he says, and holds out a hand. He's got a deep voice, too.

"Wyatt Hammer. Nice to meet you."

"And you. I hear great things about your work."

He walks us through the plans for the eatery while Natalie takes notes on the computer. As we stand at one of the unfinished counters, she shows the schematic to him on her laptop, and everything about this moment is perfectly normal, nothing special, nothing strange until a cute blonde opens the door, and walks in. Harper's friend Abby. She's holding the hand of a girl who's maybe in kindergarten. Abby works for Simon; she's his daughter's nanny, Harper told me.

The little one runs over to Simon and throws her arms around him. "Daddy! My lesson was so fun."

He scoops her up in his arms and beams, just fucking beams at his kid. "That's great, sweet pea. Will you tell me all about it the second I'm done?"

She nods and smacks her lips to his cheek, then rests her head against his, content in his arms.

I glance at Abby and say hi. She says hi to me. We've hung out a couple times, with Harper and Nick. Abby has curly blond hair and honey-colored eyes, and she's younger than Simon by maybe eight or ten years. For some reason I can't take my eyes off them. Maybe because Natalie watches them, too. There's just something about this man and this woman. Hard to say what it is, and they're not even touching.

"Hey, Abby," Simon says, and his voice reminds me of someone.

She can't seem to stop smiling as she meets his gaze. "Hi, Simon."

"How was everything today?"

"Hayden was great. We had an amazing time at the museum, and then at her lesson. I'll tell you all about it tomorrow. See you in the morning. Same time?"

"Same time."

Abby walks over to the little girl and ruffles her hair. "Bye, little sweet thing." Then she says good-bye to Natalie and me before she leaves. My potential client watches her the whole time. As she walks to the door. As she pushes it open. As she steps outside. As she waves one last time.

And I know what's in his eyes. In his voice. But I've got no room in my head to face that right now, so I do my best to zone in on work, only work, as we review the plans.

When we leave, Natalie and I stroll into the dusk of an early June evening in New York. We're both quiet for half a block or so, until she breaks the silence.

"Funny, isn't it?"

"What's funny?"

"How you can tell just by looking how he feels about her."

I stumble, losing my footing on a crack in the sidewalk. I grab onto a stoop.

"You okay?" she asks, alarmed.

I nod and brush a hand over my shirt as if I'm oh-so-cool. "Yeah. Fine."

"You sure?"

"Absolutely."

"I wonder, though," she says, as if she's musing on something.

"Wonder what?"

"How he's going to deal with the fact that he's falling in love with his daughter's nanny."

I turn to her, meet her eyes, and shrug helplessly. Because I know why his tone felt so familiar. Why his gaze gave me a sense of déjà vu. It was like looking in a mirror, seeing myself.

I speak from the most honest part of me. "I don't have a clue."

CHAPTER THIRTY-ONE

I wake up the next morning to several messages on my phone.

The first is from the bank. A huge deposit has been made in my business account. I do like dollar signs, and this one has lots of zeros with it. Scratching my head, I'm not quite sure what to make of it until I see the next message.

From Lila.

I don't mean to be presumptuous, but the job is back on so I took the liberty of paying you the deposit. Let me know when you can get back to Vegas to work on the penthouse.

My eyes widen as I start to process what this means.

Then, I find a text from Natalie.

Natalie: Did you see? Are you thinking what I'm thinking?

Wyatt: You're the mind reader. Not me. Why don't you just tell me?

Natalie: With the Vegas job back on that means we can get . . .YOU KNOW!

Wyatt: Get it on again on the rollercoaster? Add the Ferris wheel to our repertoire?

Well, a man can dream. I scroll over to my news app as I wait, but before I can open it, her reply arrives. Hope rises in me. Hope that she feels the same.

Natalie: We can get annulled properly.

Oh.
Turns out she's not on the same page as I am.
Not at all.
Not in the least.
I'm a balloon punctured, all the air leaking out of me.
My phone dings with another message from her.

Natalie: This is good, Wyatt. We don't have to worry about all the paperwork and details of a New York divorce. New York is complicated. We should have thought of this before—this way is easy.

Wyatt: Why is it easy?

Natalie: When we fly back to Vegas to start the job, I'll need to be there the first day or so to help with the setup, so we can get our annulment in person. Go to the courthouse, file it ourselves, and we'll be off the books. If the judge needs to see us, we'll still be there because of work. But the bottom line is it'll be done. Just like you wanted.

I swallow and scrub a hand over my jaw. Sitting up in bed, I toss off the covers and swing my feet to the floor.

This is good, right?

It's what we've both wanted. Hell, it's what I pretty much demanded from the second I woke up in Vegas. But now it seems like we want different things. She's insanely excited to split, while the prospect of it feels like some kind of rabid animal is gnawing a hole in my chest.

* * *

That hole deepens over the next few days as I take care of a few odds and ends for clients. It persists as I work out at the gym, as I grab a beer with Chase and he tells me the leasing agent is now making him jump through more hoops for the apartment, as I volunteer with Nick at the rescue, and especially as Natalie and I prep for Lila's job in the city of sin. It's a gaping maw when we rescind the New York divorce paperwork, since it'll be easier to deal with our annulment in Vegas and we don't want the two sets of paperwork to cause confusion.

As we board the plane late one afternoon to fly to the city where we were married—the same goddamn place where we're supposed to untie that knot—that ache tunnels through my chest, leaving my organs raw and shredded.

Even with my partner-in-fun-and-work in the seat next to me, I don't want to tell jokes or share stories. I don't want to laugh. All I want is for this shitty sensation to end.

Natalie is upbeat every second, though. Somewhere over the middle of the country, she reminds me of the plan for the first day on the job.

"Okay," I say, halfheartedly.

Then she lets me know which materials will be waiting for me.

"That's fine."

And she mentions the schedule once more, including a lunch break at the courthouse on day one.

"Sounds doable," I say, my tone lackluster.

She taps her finger to her chin, regarding me from her leather seat next to mine. "You okay there, Hammer?"

I nod. "Yeah. I'm great."

She narrows her eyes and pats my leg. "Are you sure? Because it seems like you're in a funk."

I wave a hand in the air, like this is nothing.

Out of nowhere, Natalie opens her mouth wide and moos like a mad fucking cow—a long, persistent noise that makes me feel as if I've landed in a farm.

Startled, I stare with bugged out eyes. "What the . . .?"

She fixes on a sweet-and-innocent smile and says with a straight face, even as other passengers glance her way, "I've been working on my repertoire. Do you like my cow?"

And it hits me what she did and why. A laugh works its way through me, and for the first time in days, that ulcerous feeling fades momentarily. Because of her. Trying to get me out of my funk. With a farm animal sound.

Fuck, I think I'm in . . .

"But don't forget, I'm still waiting to hear the roar that you promised me," she says with a wink.

And I know precisely why I feel so crummy. Because the closer we get to Vegas, the nearer I come to losing her. She's slipping through my fingers, this woman tangled up with me in the mess we made one crazy night. Now, I want all those entanglements. I crave them. Judging from this emptiness in my chest, I fucking *need* them, because this moment with her—her sweetness, her zaniness, her upside-down sense of humor that matches mine—is the only balm to that ache.

I don't *think* anymore.

I *know*.

I'm in love with my wife.

And the thought of her becoming my ex-wife seems horribly wrong. Like philandering termites. Or a cat that won't meow. It goes against nature.

The woman I want is the woman I married. Just a few days ago I thought we shouldn't be tied like this, that we should have a fresh start. But now that I'm certain of how I feel, I don't want the two of us to end. I want us to keep going.

The only problem is she desperately wants me to be her ex-husband by tomorrow at noon.

CHAPTER THIRTY-TWO

I can fix a broken sink. I can hang a gorgeous set of kitchen cabinets. I can build a goddamn house.

These are my skills.

But knowing how to deal with sticky situations involving the opposite sex? Let's just say that's never been my stock in trade.

That's putting it mildly, right?

I suck at making the right choices when it comes to the ladies.

After a night at the Bellagio—during which I toss and turn and weigh a million options, some of which include knocking on the door to Natalie's room, saying nothing and just fucking her instead—I'm still in the same vexing spot as I was the day before.

I'm no closer to knowing the right words to speak, in the right order, at the right time. Words that won't result in me winding up in a stew of bad-luck broth.

After I shower, I pull on jeans and a button-down. I don't normally dress up in my line of work, and this is as fancy as I get. I figure, though, a man should dress with respect when he goes to the courthouse during his lunch break.

I picture a looming concrete structure with men and women in black robes doling out your fate, and I shudder. All things being equal, I'd rather avoid the courts. And if I can figure out what to say to Natalie, maybe we won't have to go.

Hey, Nat. How'd you like to date me now?

Sweetheart, I know this might sound crazy, but any chance you'd be up for staying married?

Sooooo, I was wondering . . . what would you say to just giving this a whirl? Having dinner tonight, moving in with me, and being my woman?

Yeah, like I said, my ideas all suck.

Note to self: Try to find clarity in the next few hours.

That task would be a whole lot easier if I could trust my gut when it comes to women. All I know is I love Natalie, and I need to figure out how to keep her. Ending this marriage seems like the wrong way to go about it.

I call the one woman I've always relied on—my sister. She answers on the second ring, and speaks like an auctioneer—with extreme speed. "I'm up to my elbows in red velvet cupcake batter, but I always have time for you. Just, you know, make it quick." I can hear the familiar sounds of her bakery in the background.

Pacing across the plush carpet, I spill my heart. But, you know, quickly. "Here's the thing. I'm in love with Natalie, and I don't know what to do about anything."

Josie doesn't miss a beat. "Have you told her?"

"No. What if she doesn't feel the same way?"

"That's a chance you have to take."

"But what if—"

No need to finish—Josie knows what I'm thinking. "What if she's going to screw you over? Stab you in the back? Mess with your business?"

I scowl and am about to deny that all those too scary and too real possibilities have entered my mind, when there's a loud, wet plop on the phone line. I hear the muffled voice of my sister, then silence reigns.

I have the distinct feeling Josie's phone is bathing in a cake tub right now.

* * *

Natalie: Remind me that this is the right decision.

Charlotte: Oh, sweetie. I know it's not easy.

Natalie: But this is the right decision, right?

Charlotte: I can't make that choice for you. Part of me thinks you're crazy. But I support you, even if I don't agree with you.

Natalie: I know. I appreciate that. But what if I mess things up worse?

Charlotte: You're taking a chance. A big chance. You have to consider all the risks. Ask yourself if you have.

Natalie: I think I have. I have to do this, Charlotte. I *have* to.

* * *

I knock on Natalie's door with something not quite like butterflies flapping in my chest. Not exactly humming-birds flying around, either. It's more like crazed black crows swarming me from the inside out.

I inhale, trying to center myself, but the breath flees my lungs when she answers.

Jesus Christ, why does she have to be so gorgeous?

She wears an orange sundress with slim straps, one of those little croppy-sweater things, and a pair of beige strappy sandals. It's bright, cheery, and beautiful without being provocative.

It's so her. Sunshine and all-American apple pie dreams.

She gestures to her summery outfit. "It's my annulment dress. What do you think?"

I hate it.

I hate that she has one, that she calls it that, and most of all, that she's so damn excited to sever ties. But she's fucking stunning as she looks at me with a smile that slays me, and all I can say is the cold, hard truth. "I love it. You look gorgeous."

She taps her finger against a button on my white dress shirt. "And you look handsome." She hikes her bag up her shoulder and says in a playful tone, "What do you say we go to work, take a lunch break to split up, and maybe, if you play your cards right, we can have dinner tonight?"

That was one of my options, but now that she's given it voice, it barely seems enough. We're beyond that. We're already more. I just need to convince her.

But I'm not so pig-headed that I'm turning down a date with Natalie, so I say yes.

Beaming, she taps her watch. "We need to be at Lila's in thirty minutes, and I bet we'll be early if we leave now.

We've got time to stop for a cup of coffee on the way. Like a starter date, maybe," she says, jutting up her shoulder and looking thoroughly adorable as she flirts with me.

And that's it. I snap. I can't just date her. I can't flirt with her right now.

"I don't want coffee," I say roughly.

"What do you want then?"

"You."

A naughty smile tugs at her lips. "For old times' sake?"

"No." My tone is serious. "For new times' sake, Natalie." My heart races like a cheetah. I swallow and push past the nerves and the wild crows. "I want you. I want to be with you. I'm crazy about you," I say, starting with what's in my heart, even though there's so much more to say.

But before I can tell her more, she swallows, and tears well in her eyes. She presses her fingers to my lips.

"Shh. Don't say it."

I furrow my brow. "Don't say what?"

"Don't say anything. Not now." Her voice breaks. "Please."

She shakes her head as a tear slips down her cheek, and maybe this is why I don't understand women. Because I'm thoroughly fucking confused. She was flirty and sweet a few minutes ago, and I was sure she wanted to have a go at a relationship. Now, she's sad after I've told her I'm mad about her. I don't have a clue what to do next, but all I know is I'm not the kind of man who can stand by and watch a woman cry. "What can I do to make you happy?"

She steps closer and whispers, "Make love to me."

Now that . . . that I can do.

I cup her cheeks in my hands, push her to the wall by the door, and rake my gaze over her from head to toe, memorizing every curve, every muscle, every dip and valley. I don't know the blueprint to how we'll come together. I don't know what happens next. But I'm crazy for her.

Running my hands from her shoulders down her arms to her waist, I imprint the feel of her. She's mine, and she's the one I can't let get away.

Even though I have no answers, at this moment, I'm certain Natalie and I are on the same page. This is where we've never had any questions. I kiss her earlobe, tugging it between my teeth. She wraps her arms around my neck, pulling me closer. "You feel like mine," I whisper.

She bites her lip, as if she's holding in her words. I nuzzle her neck, kissing the column of her throat, winding her up. Her moans grow louder, higher, and I lift her skirt while her busy hands yank down my jeans. This is all I need this second—nothing more, nothing less than this connection.

She wraps her hands around my cock, and I tremble. God, she feels so fucking good. She strokes me, and I close my eyes, rocking my hips into her soft hand. "Nat," I groan, but I say no more. The lady has spoken. She wants me speechless, and she can have me speechless.

As long as she'll have me.

Her nimble hands tighten around my shaft, and she brings me closer to her. I tug down her panties and glide my fingers across her slick heat. She's ready for me. So fucking wet and lush. "Look how turned on you get," I groan, because it's too hard to stay silent.

"Wyatt. You need to stop talking and start fu—" But she stops herself, bringing her face close, her forehead touching mine, and she whispers once more, "Making love to me."

There it is again. Those two words. She's never said them to me before today—*make love*—and they let me believe she might feel the same.

I rub the head of my cock against her, and in one fast motion, I push inside. She's so wet and tight and snug, and I love the way we fit. Like we're meant to be. Like everything that happened before has led to *this*.

I want to tell her everything, how I feel, and what I want—her in my life as so much more.

"Sweetheart," I whisper in her ear, and she shudders.

"Oh, Wyatt." Her sweet voice is a bare whimper, and that sound touches down deep in my heart.

She clutches my shoulders as I make love to her. Even though the clock is ticking, even though this won't last long, I take my time in my own way. I savor every sound she makes, every sweet, sexy noise, every murmur, and every sigh. I hike her leg higher around my waist and swivel my hips deeper into her. With my touch, I want to erase whatever sadness she feels.

I might have made some bad choices. I might have made some mistakes. But this isn't one of them. She's not going to be my checkered past. She's my present, and she's my future, I know that. I believe that.

Because there's sex, there's fucking, there's lust.

And then, there's *this*. Right now. And it's everything, because I'm so in love with her.

In mere seconds, she grabs my ass and calls my name, and I'm right there with her. Our sounds are white-hot noises, wild groans, and intense cries of pleasure as she comes, and I join her in what I hope is the start of something new.

* * *

While she's in the bathroom cleaning up, I flop down on her bed, thumbing through my phone, and see that my sister texted me.

Josie: Sorry. Phone took a swan dive into the batter. Anyway, listen . . . love is all about taking a chance. It's not rocket science. Just speak from the heart, and tell her she's the one.

I smile, and a sense of calm floods my body.

Wyatt: I can do that. I can definitely do that.

Josie: Of course you can. Just trust yourself. Your new instincts with her, not the old ones.

Wyatt: Promise. I'm a new man.

I put my phone in my pocket, take a deep breath, and wait for the woman I love. The sink is running, so she's still in the bathroom. As I stand up, I wander past the TV console. Her phone buzzes on the wood. Glancing down, I see a 917 number on her screen. Someone from New York is calling her. It's not my job to answer it, so I leave it alone and the buzzing stops.

Then it rattles, like the caller has left a voicemail. The sound draws my attention back to the screen for the sliver of a second.

That's enough time for the message to flash. It's been translated from voice into text. I should look away. I really should. But I don't.

"... *Rhonda Hafner from Hafner and Hickscomb, following up on our meeting. I reviewed the information you sent, and yes, you have a reasonable claim* ..."

I grab the wall as the floor buckles. What the hell? My head swims, and a strange, new nausea whips through me. I'm even sicker when I click on my phone, run a quick Google search, and find that Hafner and Hickscomb is an employment and labor law firm in New York City.

As panic thickens in my veins, I cycle through our conversations about lawyers. When the Easy Out service fell apart, Natalie mentioned talking to an attorney friend of Charlotte's, someone specializing in family law. She said the woman gave her useful guidance on an annulment versus a divorce in New York. At the farmer's market, we even talked about not needing attorneys, and we agreed to keep our split shark-free.

By all accounts, we don't need a lawyer today.

And that's when the coldness in my veins turns to dread. My memory latches on to the dinner party, to Charlotte shushing Spencer, to me realizing that Natalie and her sister have secrets.

Big secrets. Maybe the lawyer they talked to was never the family law one. Maybe Natalie's making a case for something else.

I stab the *about us* section on the website, and that's when the knife slices through my back. The firm specializes in employment cases of class action, discrimination, whistleblowers, and sexual harassment.

Natalie didn't hire an attorney to divorce me. She hired an attorney to sue me.

"Oh shit," I mutter, with a palpable fear in my voice as I put two and two together, since I can only get them to add up to this—sexual harassment. That's why she hired an employment lawyer to make a claim.

A reasonable claim.

She'll have the text messages, too, the whole exchange about a boss falling for his employee. And that same employee lost other work because of that boss. She can't be suing the dojo. She doesn't have a contract with the dojo. She has a contract with me.

My stomach plummets, and I silently curse myself.

I did it again. I mixed business with pleasure. And this time, the results may be disastrous. This time, it's not my bad luck with women. The fault is one hundred percent on me, and this is so much worse than a poisoned sandwich.

I should have gone cold turkey on Natalie a long time ago.

CHAPTER THIRTY-THREE

I do my best to hide the rampant fear that races through me as we stop at Lila's on the way to the courthouse. I have half a mind to avoid Lila and Natalie, but after the trouble we had with this job before, I can't be a no-show. Besides, I might need Lila's money now more than ever. I couldn't be happier that Natalie and I are filing in three hours. I wish I could speed up the process.

The clock ticks loudly in my ear with every passing second as we review the plans for the kitchen remodel.

I'm focused as we talk, narrowing in on the job, not on the woman I just screwed who's going to try to screw me. I won't let her. I texted Chase that I need to talk to his cousin again, and I'm sure as soon as my buddy finishes removing a hairbrush from an eardrum or a thimble from a belly button, he'll ring me.

"We should have it done in a few weeks," I say crisply. Tension winds in me so goddamn tight I might snap any second.

"I'm so thrilled this worked out," Lila says, and drops a hand on Natalie's shoulder. "And this woman deserves all the credit. Getting to know her during the self-defense class helped me realize that I wanted this remodel to happen, and how we could make it work. I was scared, but she encouraged me."

My eyes widen to the size of the ocean. "Did she, now?"

Lila nods. "She has your back."

"I bet she does," I say, and the picture comes into even clearer focus. Natalie must have worked her ass off to get this job for us, maybe to try to claim she's running my business, too.

Fuckity, fuckity, fuckity. What a sneaky little pussycat she is. Slinking into everything. Jumping into every god-damn bag.

"Oh, Natalie. Don't let me forget to show you the closet," Lila says with a bright smile.

Natalie sets a hand on my arm. "Lila was raving about the closet here during a self-defense class last week, and I've been dying to see it."

As Lila scurries her to the closet, all I can think is I'm an hour closer to ending this fucking union with the woman I just fucked.

* * *

The mustached clerk with wire-rimmed glasses takes the papers, staples them together, and stamps them with the date.

"These will be filed today, and we'll notify you in a few weeks when the annulment has been granted," he says, without raising his face. His one-note voice should grate on my ears, but it sounds like sweet music because I'm one step closer to slicing this woman out of my life.

Natalie bounces on her toes. "Thank you so much," she says, and no one, not even Mr. Clean himself, could wipe the grin off her face. She's so happy to be splitting up, and it's irksome. Suspicious. Another piece of evidence against her.

I tap my fingers against the worn wood of the clerk's counter. "How long does this take?" I ask Bored Man.

"A few weeks," he drones.

"But on average is a few weeks one week, two weeks, three weeks, four?"

Slowly, like it costs him something to lift his chin, he looks up. "A few weeks," he repeats, which loosely translates to *shut the fuck up*.

"But what is that generally speaking?"

He gives me a you've-got-to-be-kidding-me stare. "It's more than a day and less than many days."

I sigh, but like a dog with a bone, I won't let up. "Can you ballpark, please?"

Natalie grips my bicep. "Wyatt," she says, gently, "he said a few weeks."

"But I would like to know what *a few weeks* means," I say to her. She swallows and looks away from me. I turn back to the guy, trying honey instead of vinegar. "I would be so grateful if you could give us a rough estimate? Just narrow it down a tiny bit more, pretty please?"

I fold my hands together, as if in prayer, hoping he gets that I'm pleading, and that he'll show mercy.

He parts his cracked lips once more. "Here's a rough estimate," he says, fixing on a simpering smile. "A few weeks."

He shoves a copy of the papers at us, rings the silver bell at his stand, and calls out "next."

We walk along the hallway of the courthouse, heading to the exit. "Hey. Want to tell me what that was all about?" Natalie asks.

Dragging a hand through my hair, I mumble, "Just want this whole damn thing over."

"Well, yeah," she says, rolling her eyes. "That's obvious."

"Don't try to act like you don't feel the same," I spit out as we reach the exit.

I push open the door, holding it for her. Manners still matter even when everything else falls apart.

She walks into the bright sunlight of the Vegas afternoon, placing her hand above her eyes to shield them. "You wanted it," she says coldly. "You wanted this."

I frown. "What?"

"You made it clear from the start how much you wanted this, Wyatt," she says, and now her tone is exasperated. With me. She tosses up her hands. "I thought you'd be happy. I thought this is what you wanted. Why aren't you happy?"

"You think I should be happy?" I toss back at her, frustration bubbling up, rising to the surface. I'm waiting for her to strike. I need to be ready for her ambush.

"I thought we were going to date?"

"You'd like that, wouldn't you?" There's way more vitriol in my tone than I intend.

She backs away from me. Holds up both palms in a clear "*don't touch me.*" Stares at me as if I'm someone she doesn't even know.

Her blue eyes study me before she speaks. In them I see horror reflected at me. She's horrified at me. "Why are you being so awful?" Her voice breaks. "I did this because you wanted it. You made me pro—"

Then she clasps her hand to her lips.

Her words tickle something in the back of my mind. Faint words, and I strain to hear them. Bits and pieces play in my head, and they feel like *mine*. Like things I said to her the night we married. As a song played. Our song.

Promise me, promise me, promise me.

What the hell did I ask her to do?

And now it's my turn to search her face. Her lip quivers, and her eyes are wet, as if she's holding back tears. That ache I felt for days returns, burrows into me, as if the animal that carved that hole is trying to tell me something. That maybe Natalie's not the cause of my doubt. Perhaps she's the end of it.

Rubbing a hand over my neck, I try to figure out what this moment means. And more importantly, what I believe to be true. Seeing her earnest eyes and her honest face, I don't know how she could possibly be planning to screw me over. I don't know how she could be stabbing me in the back. This woman—she's not like that.

Call it a gut instinct.

Call it a feeling.

It's true.

The question now is can I listen to it? If I was burned before, does that mean I'll be burned again?

A reel of images flickers in my mind—all our times together, right down to that moo on the plane. Even though that damning voice mail message made me want to run, my heart is telling me I've gotten it all wrong. My heart is telling me to stay.

Just because I don't trust easily doesn't mean I shouldn't believe this woman. If there's anyone I should trust, it's Natalie. And if I don't try to fix this now, I'll lose her. That's a chance I can't take, proof or not.

I go out on a limb.

"Nat, I'm sorry," I say softly, reaching for her. "I'm just a mess right now. But I'm crazy about you, and I don't want this to end," I say, and it's a start. It's the only start I can manage right now.

"I didn't, either."

Didn't.

"But you do now?" I ask, my voice wavering.

"I don't like the way you just talked to me."

My heart sinks. Here on the steps of the courthouse, she's going up, I'm heading down. I reach for her arm, wrap my hand around it. "Is this how it ends?"

My voice barely sounds like my own.

Hers is a whisper, too. "You tell me."

I want to ask about the voicemail, the call, the lawyer. I want to ask what I promised her. I want to know if I've fucked this up beyond repair. Most of all I want to know if there's a chance of fixing it.

But before I can speak again, she raises a hand. "I can't talk to you right now. We can talk later, if you decide you can treat me the way you always have, not the way you just acted. And I really hope you can do that. But right now, I need a break. I've done something crazy and probably foolish. So I'm going to go and see Lila about her closet, because that will take my mind off the email you're about to receive."

She marches down the steps and hails a cab that takes her away from me.

CHAPTER THIRTY-FOUR

There's no email.

I keep checking for whatever she's sending me, between requesting an Uber and calling Lila to ask if she wants me to head over to work now.

Her voice is sweet, but firm. "Why don't you take the afternoon off? I'm with Natalie, and we've got a few things to do."

In the background, I swear I can hear Natalie cry. The sound of it twists my chest. I wish I could comfort her, but I'm not the one she wants to be with right now.

"Okay. Take good care of her, please."

"Of course. And come back later," Lila adds, then more softly, "Sometimes a woman just needs a few minutes alone."

"Thank you." Even though my heart is torn by my own stupidity, a brief calm descends on me thanks to Lila's advice. The woman has always been good to us. She'll look out for Natalie while I figure out how to sort out the mess I made. I hang up and check my email again. Nothing.

The whole afternoon looms ahead of me like a giant black hole. I want to work, to hammer, hang, and drill, not roam aimlessly around a city I barely know, all because I'm a pigheaded idiot.

But as the driver swings onto the Strip on his way to the Bellagio, I realize this isn't just a city I barely know. This is the city where I started this love affair with Natalie, and it's the city where I don't want us to end.

I lean forward and ask the driver if we can change the destination.

"Sure thing. Where to?"

"Give me one minute to find the address," I say, doing a quick search on my phone.

I find it, and he enters it in his GPS.

Ten minutes later, I walk up to a small chapel, looking for a guy in a gold leisure suit. I want to ask Larry if he remembers my wedding. If he can help me figure out where I screwed up. It's a straw, but it's the one I'm grasping at.

Once I enter the chapel, though, and hear the music, I'm whipped back in time to my wedding night, when Elvis crooned of how he couldn't help falling in love.

And as that most romantic of romantic songs plays again, the notes somehow unlock the faint words that were tickling the back of my mind a mere hour ago. The drunken blur of my wedding ceremony is no longer a haze. It's clear, and I can hear everything I said after the vows.

I stumble into a pew as the memory crashes into me like a tsunami.

I stand at the altar, clasping her hands, looking into her eyes as Elvis soundtracks our ceremony.

"You're beautiful, Nat, and every day when I see you at work, I think how much I love coming into the office and

working with you. But it's not just because you're gorgeous. You make my business better." I grip her hands harder, holding tight, making sure she knows even in my intoxicated state that everything I say comes from my heart. "You make the business fun, but you also make it really fucking good. Without you, it's nothing."

She shakes her head, but she can't stop smiling. "That's not true. You're so talented."

Elvis sings about fools rushing in, and that word—fools— sticks with me. I don't want to be fooled again. I can't take that chance.

"No. It is true. You turned WH around, and I can't thank you enough. And I'm so fucking lucky that we get to keep working together. You want to, right?"

She nods, laughing. "Of course. Why? You're not going to fire me tonight, are you?"

I sway closer, plant a sloppy kiss on her mouth, and tell her no. "No. No. No. No fucking way am I firing you. But you've got to know that work is why we can't stay married. I've had the best time with you, and I want so much more, but we have to get an annulment in the morning."

Her eyes are intensely serious even as she hiccups. "Duh. Of course."

Then, I thread my fingers more tightly through hers. "This night has been incredible, and a part of me feels just like this song because I kinda can't help falling in love with you." Her eyes widen in surprise, and maybe even hope, but I power through with the rest of the unplanned thoughts that I've simply got to share now. "But when that happens, Nat, I make mistakes and fuck up, and I screw myself over by being foolish and too trusting. I've gotten burned. So don't let that happen to me. I want us to keep working together. Don't you?"

"Yes, God yes."

"Then promise me something."

"What is it?"

"Promise me we'll end this tomorrow. That you'll divorce me. I'll probably ask you to stay with me because I'm already crazy about you. I'll probably ask you a ton of times. I'll try everything to convince you, but I need you to promise me, no matter how convincing I am, that we'll end the marriage. Because I can't mix business and pleasure. It's my Achilles' heel, and I need you to help me. Promise me, promise me, promise me," I say, with a harsh swallow, and then I wait.

But not for long.

Her eyes are full of truth as she answers solemnly.

"I promise, Wyatt. I promise. I promise. And I get it. I do. I really do."

I drop my forehead into my palm as everything snaps into twenty-twenty hindsight. That's why she stuck to her guns. Because I asked her to. Hell, I begged her to have my back for me. I made her swear she'd keep to the plan. I even said as much to her once again on the day I ripped up her check.

I made you a promise, and I goddamn intend to stick to it, whether I had a few beers or not. I'm a man of his word, and I sure as hell expect the people I work with to treat me like it, and to act the same way.

She held to the promise I asked her to keep. She protected me from me. But now I'm the one breaking other promises to her. Unspoken ones that came in the way we kissed, in the times we shared, in the way we were so good together.

Gripping the pew in front of me, I stand up, nearly bumping into a man in a gold jumpsuit.

"Hey there. You looking to get married today, son?"

I don't answer him because my phone buzzes, and at last her email makes landfall. It's from her attorney, but she's copied on it, and the words are hers. With the fastest swipe in human history, I open the note and read the last thing I expected to see.

Dear Wyatt,

Please accept this as my letter of resignation. I have loved every moment of working with you. It's been fun, challenging, and wildly productive. But I can't work with you if I want to be with you. And I do. I really want to be yours. So I'm going out on a limb and making the choice that will let us be together. I checked with an employment attorney to make sure I wasn't breaking my contract with you, and she said in certain circumstances, when you have a reasonable claim, you can terminate employment without giving two weeks' notice. Seeing as I'm in love with you, please accept this as my reasonable claim to leave my post at WH. Effective immediately.

Love,
Natalie

Boy, did I ever fuck up.

When I look up from the screen and meet Larry's expectant gaze, the question he just asked registers fully.

And I know how to try to fix this mess I've made.

Sometimes you just have to bet the house.

CHAPTER THIRTY-FIVE

In my line of work, I've developed a specialty: the remodel.

Giving a kitchen a thorough makeover is my key skill. I know which materials I need and the right tools to use, and I've become a master at meeting a deadline.

This might be the toughest remodel I've ever attempted, though, given the wrecking ball I used on our union earlier today. But I quickly assemble a list of materials and then round them up, starting at the New York-New York hotel.

Once inside the doors, I run.

Okay. Not true.

If I ran, security would likely tackle me.

But I definitely trot. Through the casino, along the shops, up the escalator, and past the arcade, glancing longingly at the black curtain that hides the pinball machine. I don't go for the entrance. Instead, I head to the exit of the ride.

A bunch of rollercoaster riders pours out, windswept and hopped up on the adrenaline of a loop-de-loop upside-down trip.

This is where Natalie and I had our first adventure, and as I arrive at the picture counter, I'm ready and determined to find the evidence of it. The original is safe and sound at my home. Thankfully, the same woman who worked that night is here today—the cheerful brunette with pigtails and red glasses, only today her hair is yanked into a high ponytail.

"What can I do for you?" She flashes a friendly grin.

I follow Chase's advice once more—do the opposite of what I did earlier. Instead of spraying my frustration on her, as I did the clerk, I sprinkle sugar on my request. "Hey there. About two months ago I was here with the woman I've just realized I'm madly in love with."

The brunette's eyes light up, and I continue, giving her the date and the approximate time. "We had our photo taken, and our number was sixteen. If there's any chance you could find it and print me a copy, I'd be incredibly grateful and will happily pay double, triple. You name it. I need this picture, though, to show her how good we can be together."

The brunette clasps both hands over her heart. "I love this city. Vegas is full of stories of love." She straightens and adopts a serious demeanor. "I will absolutely, positively find it for you."

Ten minutes later, I walk out of New York-New York with a copy of Natalie and me at the top of the roller-coaster, riding high on our exhilaration in each other.

Next, I pop into a drugstore on the corner, use my phone to search for a photo online, email it to myself, and print it out. I buy two frames. Then I stop at the Wynn, and twenty minutes later, I have all the materials I need for one helluva redo.

The only thing left is *her*.

With a whole new fleet of nerves docking inside me, I call Natalie.

Her phone rings, and rings, and rings, then her voice-mail plays. A momentary bout of worry touches down as I wonder if she's avoiding me. But I shrug it off and dial Lila.

"Hi, Wyatt."

"Hey, I'm looking for Natalie. Is she around?"

"She is, but we're busy shopping. Give us a little bit longer, and I think she'll be ready."

"Where are you?"

She laughs. "Oh, Wyatt. Natalie's just helping me with a few items I need to get organized, and she's having quite a good time here. Don't you worry. We'll see you soon."

And I grin as I hang up.

Yes, you will.

I've got a feeling I know where the woman I want is. Because I know her. I know what she loves.

* * *

She told me she could happily live here. That this is her favorite place in the universe.

And since she's helping Lila with her closet, call me Sherlock, but I'm pretty damn sure I'll find Natalie inside this big box not too far from the Strip.

When the cab drops me off, I say a quick prayer to the universe that I can find her and take not only one step, but all the steps to fixing us. As the doors slide open, I scan The Container Store, hoping for a glimpse of blond hair, a hint of strong legs, a flash of orange summer dress.

That dress. My God, that dress. My mouth waters as I think about how she looked in it and why she was so god-damn happy today at the courthouse. Because she was giving me everything she thought I wanted. Because she loves me.

She fucking loves me.

I head down the aisle, swinging my gaze from side to side at the sea of Tupperware, hatboxes, cloth file cabinets, cat food containers, ornament holders, shower caddies, laundry baskets, pill holders in every size imaginable, hangers, and garment bags, and at last I arrive in the land of closet organizers.

Orange.

I see orange.

And it looks like happiness to me. Like all my favorite memories and everything I want for my future.

Her back is to me, and she holds a shoe drawer, showing it to Lila. "And then you use this on the middle shelf and it helps sort all your shoes," Natalie says, and her voice fills me with hope.

I hope I haven't lost her. I hope I can pull this off. I hope she doesn't think I'm crazy.

Lila meets my eyes, her own lighting up, but she quickly schools her expression. Natalie must sense I'm here, though, because she spins around in a heartbeat, obviously surprised.

And I stop thinking, and hoping, and wondering. I just *do.*

I walk up to her and speak from the heart. It's not rocket science to tell her she's the one. "I should have done a lot of things differently, Nat. I should have told you I love you first. Because I do. I love you like crazy, and maybe sometimes it makes me crazy." One corner of her lips quirks up, as if she's trying to rein in a smile. "I shouldn't have filed for the annulment today. I shouldn't have been a dick to you on the steps outside the courthouse when you were simply doing the most ridiculous thing I ever asked you to do. And most of all, I should never have asked you to keep such an unfair promise the night we married."

"It's okay, Wyatt," she says, and her voice is feathery soft. "I kept it because it mattered to you."

I shake my head, pissed at myself again, but even more in love with this woman. Lila takes a few steps back, giving us space as I continue, "I barely remembered our ceremony, let alone all those things I said to you. And that's no excuse, but it is true. I remember them now because I went back to the chapel this afternoon, and that song was playing. *Can't Help Falling in Love*. I know I felt it that night, and I feel it a million times more now." She moves closer to me, and that emboldens me. So does the expression on her face—soft and caring, then the words she mouths. *Me, too.* I want to kiss her, but I have so much more to say. "I'm not drunk now. I'm completely stone-cold sober, and I'm asking you for a second chance. I'm wildly, madly, insanely in love with you, and I brought this picture to remind you of how amazing we are together."

Her eyes twinkle as I hand her the photo. "No, you didn't bring my *O* face," she says, mad, but not mad. She's playful again, and I love that tone in her voice.

I can't help but grin. "It's much more than your *O* face, sweetheart. This," I say, pointing to the picture in the cardboard frame. "This is you and me. This is how we are together. I brought this to remind you that this is where we started. That night. On that ride. And I want this to be us." Her lips quiver, and her eyes shine with the start of tears. "I want us to keep riding the rollercoaster. To get on it over and over again. To keep climbing, and falling, and flipping upside-down, even if it makes us sick or crazy. I want to feel all the joy and exhilaration with you. The ups and downs. Because loving you is some kind of wild ride, and I don't want it to stop."

She presses her hands to my chest, gathering the fabric of my shirt. Her voice is laced with emotion, and she's on the edge of tears. "Wyatt, I only pushed the annulment because I promised I would. I did it because I love you. Because I thought you wanted it. Because I know how much promises matter to you. That's why I was crying in the hotel room earlier. Because I knew I had to do it, but I didn't want to. And I do love you. I love you so much that I can't stay mad."

I run my hand down her bare arm, unable to resist touching her. Gooseflesh rises in my wake. I breathe a sigh of relief. "But I need to confess something. Before we left your room this morning, I saw that law firm name flash on your screen. The one who sent your letter later on."

Her gaze turns quizzical. "You did?"

I nod, take a gulp, and come clean. "I freaked out and thought it meant something else. Something bad. And that's why I was such a dick at the courthouse. But then I realized how ridiculous that was well before you even sent your email. Only this time, I didn't need to see the home-less guy eat the sandwich to know it was safe. Because I know you, and I know your heart. I just hope I haven't messed things up too badly because of how cold I was."

Her grip on my shirt tightens. Her gaze is fierce and loving. "You haven't. Not at all. I swear." Then she says, with a playful cackle, "But I fully intend to prank you with a sandwich someday."

I laugh lightly. "You better. But even if I screwed things up a little, I want to make them *a lot* right. Because this can be us." I tap the photo one more time. "And we can be this couple, too," I say, drawing a fueling breath as I reach into the bag from the drugstore and take out a framed photo of two gibbons swinging on a branch in a tree.

She laughs. "You want us to be . . . gibbons?"

I reach for her hand. "Nat, did you know gibbons are one of the few animals who mate for life?"

"Along with termites, beavers, and swans," she adds, with a happy shrug. "I looked it up. It seemed like something you'd enjoy knowing."

My heart does a wild dance—because she wanted to know, and she wanted to share. "I said I was asking for a second chance, and I meant it," I say, my gaze holding hers. "But not just a dating chance. Not just a let's-go-to-dinner chance. I'm not betting a five-dollar chip on red."

I get down on one knee, and her eyes widen. I was nervous before, but I'm not anymore. I've never been so sure of what I want and what I need. "I'm going all in, and I'm asking you for a second chance at marriage. I want to go home to New York and live with you and share a life with you, and I want you to be my wife. Let's stay married. Hell, let's get married again. Let's renew our vows. Marry me over and over. Every year. Let's make it our thing."

Her eyes turn to moons, and her jaw falls open. "Oh my God," she gasps.

I take out the gift I bought at the Wynn—at the fancy jewelry shop in the fanciest hotel. I open the blue velvet box and show her a two-carat emerald-cut solitaire.

"Be my gibbon," I say with wild hope.

She falls to her knees, throws her arms around me, and kisses me like she wants all the same things. It's only been a few hours without kissing her, but hell, it's so damn good to do it again, to feel her lips on mine where they belong. When she breaks the kiss, she meets my gaze, and says softly, sweetly, "I'll be your gibbon. But don't you know, I already am?"

The smile that is my greatest joy spreads across her beautiful face, and I can't believe how lucky I am. "Oh, and about that letter of resignation you sent me," I begin, tapping my chin. "I had another idea."

"Tell me," she says, practically bouncing. But then she stops, and her smile disappears as she looks at her watch. "Wyatt," she whispers, in that soft kind of voice that portends trouble. My heart speeds up.

"What is it?"

"We need to go. The courthouse is closing. They're filing our annulment paperwork."

I grab her hand and tug her up. "I don't want this marriage to be annulled."

"I don't either."

Lila chimes in. "Let's take my car. It feels like something a fairy godmother would do."

And, you know, that pretty much describes her role in this story. We rush out of the store, slide into her sleek black car, and peel away.

CHAPTER THIRTY-SIX

"Ohhhhhhhhh."

The clerk gives a double-shouldered shrug. "I am just so, so sorry." His tone tells me he's not sorry at all.

"You see," he says, tilting his head, "since you were in such a hurry, I took a second look at your paperwork. You'd been so thoughtful as to leave a note explaining that you'd tried to file with Easy Out Divorce. And"—he clears his throat as if he's prepping to deliver a punch line —"since Easy Out Divorce is now a known scammer, the courts have a temporary offer that anyone who was scammed by Easy Out can get a special, fast annulment. So I fast-tracked it for you. Isn't that swell?"

"You did?" I ask, as my shoulders sag.

The clerk clasps his hands together. "It's with great pleasure that I tell you your annulment was granted today, and this marriage has been dissolved."

My heart sinks.

But only for a second. Because where there's a will, there's a way. "No problem," I say with a smile. This time, I'm practicing being a good guy. Because good guys win.

And this good guy knows there's more than one tool to fix something broken.

I turn to Natalie. "Want to bet there's a city hall or someplace like that where we could get married again? Let's do it right. Do it now."

Her eyebrows rise, and she asks the clerk where civil ceremonies are performed.

He points up. "Sixth floor. Office of Civil Marriage Unions." He hands us the papers and calls out *next*.

After we snag a marriage license, ask Lila to be our witness, and confirm our early evening walk-in appointment, Natalie and I stand in front of a judge in his office chambers, and we get married again.

This time it's simpler.

This time we're sober.

There's no twenty-four-hour chapel, or sorta Elvis impersonator. Just my wife and me, sealing our love once more. I don't ask her to undo it tomorrow, because I want to be entangled with her forever when we say I do.

Then, I kiss my bride in our second marriage, even though it's our first legally. But who cares about technicalities when my lips are on hers? She tastes so lovely, and I'll never tire of kissing her. My head spins from the sweetness of her mouth, and my body lights up from this connection we share. "You're stuck with me now," I say when our lips separate.

With her hands looped around my neck, she murmurs, "That's where I want to be."

As we head down the steps of the courthouse into the sunset of this city, leaving Lila on her own, I flash back to the moment here earlier today, when we were falling apart.

I reach for her arm. Wrap my hand around it. "Hey, let's make this the end of us ending. What do you say to that?"

She grips my hand. "It had better be the end of breaking up."

I run my fingers along the back of her dress. "I guess it's not your annulment dress anymore."

She gestures to the orange fabric. "It's my wedding dress. And truth be told, I wore it today hoping something like this might happen."

"You're such a planner."

"That's why you need me."

"I do need you. And that's why I want to tell you my plan for rejecting your resignation."

She loops her arms around my neck and says, "Tell me. But make it fast, because I'd really like to consummate our marriage."

It's safe to say my proposal floors her. She cries again, and they're tears of happiness. When we make it back to my room, I kiss them away, strip off all her clothes, then mine, too.

She's naked before me, and it occurs to me that we've only made love once before without our clothes on. We've always been rushing, risking, tempting fate. The last time we were chest-to-chest, skin to skin, was on our first wedding night a few months ago.

And I don't care what the courts say about marriages being dissolved. Not existing. Never happening.

We happened, and we're happening again, so I join her on the bed. When I enter her, we both groan. Electricity shoots through me. It feels like pure bliss as I sink into her, savoring the way we fit. She moans happily and meets my gaze. It's intense, the way we look at each other. The way we *want* to look into each other's eyes.

"Can we do this every night?" she asks in a sexy purr as she wraps those gorgeous legs around my ass.

"Every morning, too," I say on a thrust, and we move together. "Want to know why?"

"Why?" she asks, as she arches her spine, her lips falling open.

"Because I love fucking my wife," I say with a throaty groan. "And I fucking love my wife."

I'm rewarded with a wild cry of pleasure, then another, and it doesn't take her long at all to fly high. Pretty soon, I'm doing that thing she loves—coming loud and hard. I might even roar.

I'd like to say we spend the night riding the rollercoaster or the Ferris wheel. But nope. We go horizontal again. All night long. It's as perfect as a wedding night can be. And I'm not just saying that because we order an Oreo sundae from room service sometime in the middle of the night.

But that is good, too. And I do like Oreos.

EPILOGUE

The ladder rests against the bright white wall in our home. Natalie balances carefully on the top rung, hanging a sign. I suppose I could do this for her, but she insisted, and the woman really does love getting her hands on the tools.

She's good with all of them, but she's particularly good with one of mine, if you get my drift.

Anyway, here's the *ladder*. See what I did there? I didn't leave you hanging. I promised a dirty ladder story, and I'm going to deliver.

She's on the ladder because she knows I like this view. Who am I kidding? I love this view. Perched on the edge of the couch in our living room, I savor the sight in front of me—my Natalie, in a little pink skirt that swishes around her thighs.

"Enjoying yourself?"

"It's *hard* to tear myself away."

She laughs then raises the hammer and taps, taps, taps until the new sign is up on the wall. We have a matching one in our office. It says Hammer & Hammer Carpentry

& Construction. We changed the name. Yes, *we*. Because it's *ours*. Everything is ours.

I've learned you need to give a little in a relationship. Or, I should say, give a lot. Natalie was willing to give up her livelihood for me. I couldn't let her do that. Instead, I found another solution. She stayed, and we run the business together as husband and wife. I still do the building; I'm the carpenter, after all. But she's the magic. She's the glue. She's made this business thrive. And it's hers as much as it's mine. We own it together. Sometimes, she slings on a tool belt and helps finish a job, but we've expanded finally, and we have employees who are reliable and show up for work.

Natalie manages it all. She makes it happen every day. "I've always loved this job. I never thought of myself as just an assistant," she'd said when I pitched her on my proposal after our official Vegas wedding.

"You've always been so much more. You've made everything at *our* company better."

"And I'll keep doing that. But I'm still teaching my classes at night," she'd said.

"I would expect nothing less from the woman who can kick my ass."

Now, she turns around, facing me, one hand holding onto the top rung as she shows me the sign—our business, our marriage, *us*. "How does it look?"

"Like it was meant to be. I love everything about it, especially the way those two names go together."

She has my heart, my body, my business, my home. Sharing the business with her barely scratches the surface of all she has given me—this unconditional love. Oh, and obviously Natalie lives with me now, which means Josie's looking for a roommate, but that's a story for another time.

For now, I've got my woman to tend to. I walk over to the ladder, climb a step, push up her skirt, and pull her panties to the side.

I kiss her and lick her and taste her until she's moaning and groaning, and sighing sexily.

That's my cue to keep her safe. "C'mon. Take my hand," I say softly, and I guide her down the ladder, scoop her up, and set her on the couch, where she spreads her legs, and I devour her sweetness.

Look, ladders are fun for foreplay, but when you're into risky sex, you've got to know which risks to take. Can't have my wife falling off a ladder because I make her come so hard.

And that's precisely what I do as she goes wild on the couch against my mouth. Then I make love to her.

Afterward, she smiles woozily at me and says, "Should we go get ready for our wedding?"

Yeah, we're *those* people. We're the ones who got married in Vegas, came home, and threw another wedding party for our friends and family. We like marrying each other.

A lot.

So we're going to do it all again. Truth be told, we'll probably renew our vows next year, and the next and the next.

ANOTHER EPILOGUE

A few months later

Once upon a time there was a man, there was a woman, and there were some wild speed bumps on the road to their happily-ever-after.

But we navigated them all.

Along the way, I discovered that trust isn't about proof. It isn't about getting fooled, or not getting fooled. It's a choice. One you make with your heart. Natalie has mine, and I had to learn that it was safe and sound in her care. Always.

Her heart is safe with me, too, even though she does like to beat me up in her videos.

Her self-defense series has become quite popular online. New students have found her through them and have started taking the classes she teaches a few nights a week. That makes her happy, and when she's happy, I'm happy, too.

She might have to cut back soon, though. Things are changing around here. Her belly is a little rounder.

No, it wasn't an *oops* baby. It didn't happen one drunken night. *Please.* My wife is a planner. And we planned this. In fact, the bun might very well have gone into her oven on our *third* wedding night. The one right here in New York.

The two of us are the first of our friends to get knocked up, but that fits us. We seem to have two speeds—either stalled or moving at sixty miles an hour. We're not stalled anymore, so in this case we broke all the limits, and in several months, we'll be a family.

Right now, though, I'm heading out with Natalie to the farmers' market. We're not shopping for asparagus or arugula. We've always liked it risky, and today we're going to take our chances.

We've got a date behind the banana stand.

THE END

Wondering if Chase will get that lease after all? Or what Josie will do about her roommate situation? Or just how tough it'll be for Chase to stop flirting with her? Find out in FULL PACKAGE, releasing in January! But before then, be sure to check out THE SEXY ONE, a swoony and sexy romantic comedy about Simon and Abby, releasing in October!

ALSO BY LAUREN BLAKELY

Check out my contemporary romance novels!

BIG ROCK, the hit New York Times
Bestselling standalone romantic comedy!

MISTER O, also a New York Times
Bestselling standalone romantic comedy!

The New York Times and USA Today
Bestselling Seductive Nights series including
Night After Night, *After This Night*,
and *One More Night*

And the two standalone
romance novels, *Nights With Him* and
Forbidden Nights, both New York Times and
USA Today Bestsellers!

Sweet Sinful Nights, *Sinful Desire* and
Sinful Longing, the first three books in the
New York Times Bestselling high-heat
romantic suspense series that spins
off from Seductive Nights!

Playing With Her Heart, a USA Today
bestseller, and a sexy Seductive Nights spin-off standalone!
(Davis and Jill's romance)

21 Stolen Kisses, the USA Today
Bestselling forbidden new adult romance!

Caught Up In Us, a New York Times and
USA Today Bestseller! (Kat and Bryan's romance!)

Pretending He's Mine, a Barnes & Noble and
iBooks Bestseller! (Reeve & Sutton's romance)

Trophy Husband, a New York Times and
USA Today Bestseller! (Chris & McKenna's romance)

Far Too Tempting, the USA Today Bestselling standalone
romance! (Matthew and Jane's romance)

Stars in Their Eyes, an iBooks bestseller!
(William and Jess' romance)

My USA Today bestselling
No Regrets series that includes
The Thrill of It
(Meet Harley and Trey)
and its sequel
Every Second With You

My New York Times and USA Today
Bestselling Fighting Fire series that includes
Burn For Me (Smith and Jamie's romance!)
Melt for Him (Megan and Becker's romance!)
and *Consumed by You* (Travis and Cara's romance!)

Sapphire Affair series…
The Sapphire Affair
The Sapphire Heist

ACKNOWLEDGMENTS

A big, huge banana stand-size thank you to my readers! YOU ARE THE REASON I WRITE! I love hearing from you, I love that you read my books, I love that you love romance. I am grateful to so many people for bringing WELL HUNG to you. Thank you to Mermaid Jen McCoy, to Cover Goddess Helen Williams, to She-Who-Shall-Not-Vacation KP Simmon, and to You-Know-Me-So-Well Kim Bias. Much gratitude to daily grind gal Kelley Jefferson, to Dena Marie, who suggested the dinner party, to Lauren McKellar, who makes it all come together, and to Candi Kane, who is a ray of sunshine and good will. Big love to my girls – Kristy, Laurelin, CD, Lili, Corinne, Vi, Kendall and many more! A massive thanks to my husband and kids! And as always, much love to my dogs!

CONTACT

I love hearing from readers! You can find me on Twitter at LaurenBlakely3, or Facebook at LaurenBlakelyBooks, or online at LaurenBlakely.com. You can also email me at laurenblakelybooks@gmail.com

40666735R10153

Made in the USA
San Bernardino, CA
26 October 2016